Devlin leaned forward, placing his elbows on his knees.

"Almost invariably in any crowd, there's at least one person who's unhinged enough to cause serious trouble."

Elaine drew a breath. "A psychopath."

Devlin shrugged. "The word for it doesn't matter. The important thing is that some people get their thrills by causing trouble."

"So what do you think you can do about it?"

"Join the party and listen."

Elaine stiffened. "You're going undercover with those guys? Are you kidding me?" Then she paused. "But that's what you do, isn't it?" She uncurled and stood up. "You just be careful you don't draw the kind of attention that'll bring trouble back to Cassie."

Then she left the room. And Devlin once again considered moving to the motel. Except now it was overfull.

Then another thought struck him. If there was any trouble out of this invasion, he needed to be here to protect Cassie, his mother and Elaine.

That came first, before anything else.

He wondered if he was being a plain fool to even think of infiltration.

CONARD COUNTY: COVERT AVENGER

NEW YORK TIMES **BESTSELLING AUTHOR**
RACHEL LEE

INTRIGUE

To Patience Bloom for many years of kindness, encouragement and great editing.

Harlequin®
INTRIGUE™

ISBN-13: 978-1-335-45690-8

Conard County: Covert Avenger

Copyright © 2024 by Susan Civil-Brown

Harlequin Enterprises ULC
22 Adelaide St. West, 41st Floor
Toronto, Ontario M5H 4E3, Canada
www.Harlequin.com

Printed in Lithuania

MIX
Paper | Supporting responsible forestry
FSC® C021394

Rachel Lee was hooked on writing by the age of twelve and practiced her craft as she moved from place to place all over the United States. This *New York Times* bestselling author now resides in Florida and has the joy of writing full-time.

Books by Rachel Lee

Harlequin Intrigue

Conard County: The Next Generation

Cornered in Conard County
Missing in Conard County
Murdered in Conard County
Conard County Justice
Conard County: Hard Proof
Conard County: Traces of Murder
Conard County: Christmas Bodyguard
Conard County: Mistaken Identity
Conard County: Christmas Crime Spree
Conard County: Code Adam
Conard County: Killer in the Storm
Conard County: Murderous Intent
Conard County: Covert Avenger

Visit the Author Profile page at Harlequin.com.

CAST OF CHARACTERS

Elaine Paltier—Conard County sheriff's deputy, widowed with three-year-old autistic daughter.

Devlin Paltier—Covert operative for the CIA, off the grid to protect his assets, one of whom has been killed. It's been years since he returned to Conard City or saw his mother.

Lu Paltier—Devlin's mother, lives with Elaine and cares for her autistic granddaughter.

Cassie Paltier—Three-year-old with autism. Has trouble with personal contact and speech.

Beggans Bixby—Ranch owner furious about UFO hunters trespassing on his land, upsetting his cattle. All for two red lights that have been there for years.

Zoe and Kalina—Two female assassins from Eastern Europe who have come to kill Devlin for his part in their brother's death.

Chapter One

Conard County Deputy Elaine Paltier drove along a dusty gravel road on her nightly round of Wyoming's isolated ranch country. Out here, excitement was rare, unless there was an accident or injury, or the weather created a problem. The mountains to the west caught the bright moonlight on their snow-capped peaks, adding beauty to gently rolling foothills and the early spring growth in the fields.

The routine, however, gave Elaine plenty of opportunity to ramble around inside her own head, allowing her to think about her life, her job and mostly her young daughter. Being a single parent had its difficulties, even with help from her mother.

She didn't mind this part of her official duties, though. Each assignment was only for two weeks before she'd be relieved by another deputy. Hardly enough time to find these patrols by herself to be boring.

That night, however, matters got exciting, although indirectly at first. She saw two glowing red spots near the Bixby ranch and wondered if they were tower markers. But who would have erected them since her last two-week tour? And if someone had, she'd have certainly heard about it.

As she got closer, the glowing areas became more orange and bigger.

"Oh, God," she muttered, her heart accelerating. A range fire? But in two different spots? She grabbed her radio to call for backup from the fire squad, but the device hissed and refused to connect. The satellite phone was no better. Dead zones in these distant areas were not uncommon, providing unreliable service that could be maddening and dangerous at times.

Uncommon or not, she had to find a way to summon help. She pressed her accelerator, driving as fast as she dared on the gravel. Range fires could explode with incredible speed, and the green spring growth would offer no protection once a fire started and dried out everything around it.

Seeing the driveway for Beggan Bixby's ranch house, she pulled a sharp right and drove even faster to warn the old rancher—maybe get a better radio signal or use his landline, too.

Were those red blobs growing larger? Elaine couldn't tell, so she turned most of her focus to the looming ranch house. She flipped on her roof lights but no siren, to warn the rancher that she was approaching. All the while, tension increasingly tightened her muscles. A serious range fire could blow up in no time at all.

Then, scaring her half to death, a man appeared in the driveway right in front of her, turning blue and white in the flash of her light bar. He held a shotgun cradled across his breast almost like a baby. Much to her relief, it was clearly cracked open. Not yet a threat.

She jammed her Suburban into Park with a spray of gravel and opened her door, leaning out. "Mr. Bixby?"

Yeah, it was Bixby, in old jeans and a work shirt, with a stained, ancient cowboy hat jammed on his head. He was stomping his feet in anger. "You finally come to get rid of 'em?"

The question put her off-balance. Not at all what she'd expected to hear. *Finally?* "You mean the fire up north of here?" She pointed at the reddish-orange balls of light as she climbed out of her vehicle.

"Hell no. I ain't talking about them."

Elaine looked from him to the glowing light, more orange now. "How can you ignore them? I don't have to tell you about range fires. I need your phone."

"'Tain't no fire."

"How can you be sure unless we go look?" As if it could be anything else. The idea of a range fire made the skin on the back of her neck crawl. A disaster that could reach hundreds of square miles in no time at all. But now she was dealing with a man who'd lost his mind somehow? She had to get to his phone.

But Bixby had a ready answer. "I see them lights a lot. Now, you just do your job and get rid of them SOBs."

She nearly gaped at him. "You want me to get rid of those lights?" How the hell was she supposed to do that without help if it was a fire? And why did he keep dismissing them, then demanding she get rid of them? "I can get a fire truck out here to put them out. But I need your landline. Radio's not working."

Bixby stomped his feet some more and raised his scratchy voice. "You damn useless cop. *Not* the red lights. They ain't no trouble. So when are you going to get rid of them?"

Elaine began to feel some serious irritation, along with a sense of having slipped out of reality. "How am I supposed to get rid of the lights if you won't let me call the fire department?"

"I been calling you guys for more 'n' a month about

this. Y'all ain't done nothing about it. I don't give a rat's patootie about the lights. I keep tellin' ya, they ain't no problem—never have been. You ever listen?"

"Then why do you want me to get rid of them?"

Bixby was clearly reaching the end of his rope. He started to shout. "I ain't talking about them lights. I keep tellin' ya! Get rid of the cussed fools crossin' my fence. I don't want no gawkers cuz of them dang lights. This ain't a ranch like the one on the TV."

Elaine sought to make the connection, then did. In an instant, she *knew* she had fallen down the rabbit hole. She spoke carefully, needing to be sure she understood before Bixby escalated beyond his current anger and frustration. "I saw that show once."

"Well, I ain't that place, and I'm getting sick of freakin' trespassers climbing my fence and bothering my herd. Damn it, I got cattle to raise."

Elaine looked to the north, saw the lights were still there but didn't seem to have grown. They didn't resemble a range fire, which by now would have been a whole lot larger. Just lights, like Bixby had said. Her tension eased as she gave her full attention back to the old man. "Bet you got gawkers tonight." The idea of people chasing balls of light amused her. Clearly Bixby didn't share that feeling.

"Hell yeah." Bixby spat on the ground. Chewing tobacco. "Swear I'm gonna shoot one or two of them soon as I get a chance. Hell, I can't afford no security guys to protect my fence and my herd. I'm it."

Elaine's stomach tightened with apprehension. "Mr. Bixby, you don't want to kill somebody and put yourself in jail."

"I got a right to shoot anybody who comes on my land."

That was debatable, and would require a judge and

maybe a jury. She realized she wasn't going to be able to talk or scare him out of murderous intent—not right now. Her hands tightened with a sense of urgency, seeking a way to calm the situation.

She glanced north again at the lights, more curious now than anything. "What are they?"

"Damned if I know. Been showin' up from time to time all my life, but they ain't hurt no one and nothing. Seems like they ain't no problem, and I'm happy to leave them alone. But things might not be so simple if them jackasses keep crossing my fence and taking pictures and all that other stuff they do. Bunch of lunatics."

Elaine sighed, now having a clear picture of the *real* problem here, and it wasn't just a couple of lights or orbs or whatever they might be called. No, it was people who wanted to climb his fence—maybe even cut it—and wreak havoc on a rancher's land and herd.

Bixby spat again and resettled his shotgun in his arms. "Used to call 'em UFOs," he said. "Now they got a new name—UAPs. Don't make no difference. No little gray or green men ever been seen. Nothin' ever seen but them balls. Bet you can't even take a good picture of one."

Elaine studied Bixby, thinking he was a little more informed than a man who simply wanted to keep trespassers out. *UAPs?*

A recent term not yet in common vernacular as far as she knew. Maybe he'd been talking to some of these trespassers. Arguing with them. Given this man, it wouldn't surprise her. Maybe the only surprise was that he hadn't killed one of them yet.

Bixby glared at her in the lights from her vehicle. "What the hell you gonna do about them, Deputy? Them trespassers. I complained before, but you never even sent anyone out here. So what are you going to do?"

Since it was unlikely that half the Conard County Sheriff's Department could come out here to guard Bixby's land from trespassers, Elaine had no answer.

Which apparently didn't surprise Bixby. "Ha," he said. "What good are all you folks? Ya think I don't pay taxes like everyone else around here?"

"It's more about manpower," Elaine said finding a reasonable response, although minute by minute, Bixby was looking closer to a frazzled edge.

"Wouldn't take many of you to convince them jerks to stay away."

Well, he had a point there. A few deputies talking to these invaders might scare them off. Briefly.

"They'll just come back eventually," Elaine said honestly.

Bixby went off into a cussing fit that would have amused Elaine a whole lot more if he hadn't been holding a shotgun.

When he ran out of words and rage and fell briefly silent, Elaine spoke heresy. "You know, Mr. Bixby, those balls of light are hardly harmless to you and this ranch if they're causing these trespassers to overrun you."

Bixby glared at her again as if she were a fool. "They didn't bring them jerks. Like I said, the lights been there on and off my whole life. Even my cattle ain't bothered by them."

Bixby spat again, and this time he cocked the shotgun and waved it. "You get yourself out of here. Useless. Just useless."

Elaine started to turn, her back prickling with awareness of that shotgun. Leaving was the only choice to avoid a possibly dangerous confrontation. She'd only taken two steps toward her Suburban when Bixby spoke again.

"I know you," he said. "Elaine Paltier, George Henley's girl. Dang, wouldn't your daddy be ashamed of you right now."

Elaine stiffened but kept walking to her vehicle, then climbed in and switched off all her flashers. Bixby could go to hell.

Yet as she swung her vehicle around to continue her patrol, she saw the red lights again. Then she saw them wink out.

She braked and waited for five minutes or so, but they never reappeared.

A mystery that would always remain a mystery, she supposed. But she had a real life to deal with, and she resumed her patrol at an easy pace. Eventually her radio and satellite phone returned to normal function.

After a few more minutes, she returned to normal as well, smiling into the night. Red lights, trespassers and Mr. Bixby.

What a story!

Chapter Two

In the morning, after Elaine had finished filing her report at the office, the laughter and snickers began to run around among the other deputies. She couldn't hide her own smile as she listened to the would-be comics filling in the blanks of her encounter with Beggan Bixby.

She had, of course, written the terse report of a police officer: name, date, time, description of complaint and her response. Bare bones. Basic.

But the other deputies in her office had no trouble imagining a scene that went far beyond the report. Elaine had to laugh along with them because they were coming close to what had actually happened. And it was ridiculous—*so* ridiculous—except for one thing.

"Guys," she said, "we still have to do something about the trespassers at the Bixby ranch."

Lev Carson hooted. "Which trespassers? The orange blobs?"

Still smiling, Elaine left as another round of laughter filled the office. She had no doubt two or three of her colleagues would head out to the Bixby ranch that day to deal with the invaders, laughter or not.

But Elaine's thoughts had already moved on. She was seriously looking forward to seeing her three-year-old daughter, who would be fresh out of bed, getting ready for her breakfast and still smelling of that sweet baby smell she hadn't yet outgrown.

Cassie made everything worthwhile. Everything.

MIDMORNING, ELAINE WAS still yawning her way through her third cup of coffee and Cassie was still in her pajamas having splashed milk from her cereal onto a coloring book. The damp spots and curling paper didn't bother Cassie a bit. With her tongue stuck out in concentration, her mop of blond curls all awry, she worked on a unicorn that filled the entire page. Cassie's choice of colors was bold and on the wild side.

Her late husband's mother, Lu, had gone to the grocery. Lula was Elaine's lifesaver. After Caleb Paltier's death in a construction accident, Lu had moved right in, taking charge of Cassie and the house while managing not to make Elaine feel like she had lost control. Making it possible for Elaine to continue working and paying the bills.

Except that, for a long while, Elaine hadn't cared about being in charge of anything. That was changing at last, and Lu was sliding into second place with a smile. Not that Elaine wanted Lu to feel that way, but she needed some control of her own life beyond her job. Needed to feel there was some kind of future for her and Cassie.

Then the doorbell rang. The old thing sounded more like a sick frog than a chime. Something she needed to take care of.

There weren't always enough hours in the day. Simple repairs like the doorbell had been put on hold for entirely too long. And some of them had waited because getting herself out of bed had, for a while, been a chore. The feeling still visited her sometimes, but infrequently now.

Smothering another yawn, she tugged the tie of her gray sherpa robe more tightly around herself. She wondered who it might be since most of her neighbors didn't drop by when they knew she'd been on the graveyard shift. Still, maybe someone had a serious problem. The thought brought her fully awake.

She opened the door. And stared, even though she recognized the man. But she hadn't expected to see him.

"Devlin?" she said almost uncertainly. Her late husband's brother? The last time she had seen him had been at Caleb's funeral.

"Hi, Elaine," he answered with a smile. "I guess Mom didn't tell you I was coming."

No, his mom hadn't. But so what? As her mind whirled with surprise, she realized she was being rude by not inviting him in, letting him stand there in the chilly morning air. "Come in," she said, trying to be gracious, forcing a smile. "Heavens, it's been forever!"

He entered and she stepped back, taking him in. He wore a denim shearling jacket, jeans and hiking boots. More casual than she was used to seeing him. He looked thinner, too. A lot thinner. And older, as if life had treated him roughly. Only his short dark chestnut hair appeared the same, and it was now dashed with some gray.

Devlin hardly looked like Caleb. They might have come from different families, although they didn't, but there was still enough similarity to make her heart stumble. But no, this would do no good. She yanked back from sorrow and forced her smile to widen. "Your mom went to the store, but Cassie is in the kitchen. Come on and have some coffee."

He shrugged out of his jacket and hung it on a hook near the door.

As she turned to lead the way to the kitchen, she paused. "I'm afraid Cassie won't remember you," she added, to fill a silence that might become awkward.

"I'd be surprised if she did. She was, what—eighteen months the last time I saw her?"

At the funeral. Nearly two years ago. And during that time, Devlin had sent only a few emails. Any relationship that might have grown between them had been stymied by his duties abroad with the State Department.

Of course, he'd kept in better touch with his mother— occasional phone calls, an actual letter or two. No reason he should keep in touch with Elaine. She was another part of Caleb's life he had barely been exposed to.

Devlin spent a few quiet minutes talking to Cassie, who looked slightly frightened by the big stranger, but then he had the sense to look away and leave her alone while he directed his attention to Elaine.

"Mom says your job is keeping you really busy."

She nodded as she brought him a mug of steaming coffee. "'Busy' is mostly a good thing. But I guess you know that, given *your* job."

Elaine could have sworn that he almost winced, but then his face smoothed over. "Well," he answered, "I hope you don't mind that I'll be around for a few weeks, maybe a month."

Startled, she froze as she set the mug before him. "Is something wrong?"

His mouth twisted. "There is something very wrong when my sister-in-law asks that. But you're right. I've been a stranger. And yeah, something is wrong. You can call it 'strongly recommended leave.' It seems someone decided it was high time I took a vacation."

She sat in the chair beside Cassie and eyed him. "You do something wrong?"

He shook his head. "Trust me, I did not. Nope, the chief just decided I'd saved up too much vacation time for it to be healthy. Told me to go breathe some fresh air."

At that, she gave a half smile. "It happens. So why not Tahiti or the Caribbean? Great vacation spots. Better than here." Then she bit her lip, hoping she hadn't sounded as if she wanted him to leave. She didn't want that. His mother didn't deserve that.

He looked down at his mug, then raised a face that reflected faint sorrow. "I got to thinking about Caleb. About you. About Cassie. About my mom. I've been a prodigal son for too long."

Elaine was sure Lu would agree with that. She wondered if her mother-in-law had applied some pressure to Devlin. Then, if so, why now? Why not in past years?

She nearly sighed. The law officer was taking over again, asking a bazillion questions she'd never, in this case, be able to ask out loud.

But as she sat there in the lengthening silence, a certainty grew in her. Something was definitely wrong with this trip, no matter what he said. This was not a simple visit to family.

As she drained her coffee, she remembered basic courtesy. Much as she hated to cook, she asked, "You want something to eat?"

Devlin shook his head. "I stopped at Maude's before coming over here."

Elaine rose to get more coffee. Weary or not, sitting still had suddenly become difficult. Nothing was right. She just wished she knew what was wrong.

"The diner must have been a trip down memory lane for you."

He chuckled at that. "Maude hasn't softened much, has she? And her daughter is damn near a clone. She bangs those dishes around almost as sharply as Maude does."

"A lot of us wonder how the dishes survive." Having topped off their mugs, she sat again at the table. Cassie remained totally involved in her coloring. But that was Cassie. *Special needs. On the spectrum.* God, she hated those words. Cassie was Cassie, a lovely child who had some quirks. Elaine had trouble seeing it any other way. She had certainly come to hate labels.

Especially when those labels seemed like a huge barrel into which people could toss anyone who didn't fit someone's idea of *normal*. What the hell was *normal*, anyway?

"Elaine?" Devlin spoke quietly. "Is something wrong?"

Abruptly she realized that her face had tightened into a scowl. She forced herself to brighten her expression. "Just tired," she answered. "Graveyard last night."

He raised his brows. "Then what are you doing up? Why not catch some sleep?"

She shook her head. "Best thing to do to make the switch back to days is stay up all day after I finish my last graveyard. I'll sleep tonight, and then tomorrow will be close to normal."

"Makes sense." He nodded and sipped his coffee. Then he glanced at Cassie, seeing that she was still busy coloring. "Quite some concentration there."

Elaine nearly winced. "Yeah," was all she said.

He looked down briefly as if he'd heard something in her tone, but then he raised his face with a smile. "When will Mom be back? Maybe I should just go get settled in the motel and come back later."

"The motel?" God. Elaine had no trouble imagining Lu's response to that. Well, she pretty much had the same reaction to the idea herself, just milder. "Damn, Devlin, this is your home now. You think Lu wants you sleeping at the La-Z-Rest?"

"Hardly my home," he replied. "I've been here so rarely over the last fifteen years I can barely claim the *town* as home."

And the house he'd grown up in had been sold by Lu when she moved into the Paltier house to take care of Elaine and Cassie. Elaine would have bet that Devlin didn't have much of a home for himself anywhere, not with him being overseas with the State Department. Kinda sad, even though she wasn't in much of a mood to feel sad for Devlin. Dang, the guy had taken off all those years ago and basically made a stranger of himself, even to his own mother.

But the thing that concerned her right now was her mother-in-law. "No, you stay here. You can argue about it with Lu if you want, but I won't hear of it. Get your stuff out of your car. There's a small bedroom in the back that you can have."

A room she had once shared with Caleb as an office and now was hers alone. Computer, papers, bills...all stuff that could be moved, and there was a daybed for him to sleep on.

"I don't want to impose—"

"Maybe not," she interrupted him. "But this is the way it's gonna be."

At that, he smiled again. "Total deputy," he remarked. "Giving orders."

She might have flushed, but rather than feel embarrassed, she started to become irritated. *Lack of sleep,* she told herself.

"Whatever," she said. Then she rose. "I'm going to get dressed. Cassie? Wanna come with me?"

Cassie slowly lifted her head from her coloring book and looked at Devlin, then dropped her crayon and slid off her chair. She walked beside her mother. No touching.

Well, that was as clear as a sign in flashing neon, Elaine thought as she headed for her bedroom with her daughter. The girl clearly didn't want to be alone with the stranger. She wondered if Cassie would become comfortable with Devlin. Or if she even should.

Devlin, after all, had a track record of seldom being around.

She heard him call out, "I'm going to step outside."

Good. Easier than having him in here and trying to fill in conversational blanks.

OUTSIDE, BRIGHT MIDMORNING sunlight flooded the world and the remaining chill of spring defied the greening leaves. Devlin looked around and wondered if he'd lost his mind.

Coming to see his mother, well, that was normal. Even after all this time. She'd been torn up by Caleb's death, and Devlin had done what he could to comfort her in the aftermath. But he was confined by his job's demands. By other people's lives depending on him. By information he absolutely couldn't turn over to a backup. A week. Just a week for his grief over Caleb. A week when he'd hardly left his mother's side, except to try to spend a little time with Elaine, who was grieving as much as anyone and totally absorbed in her small daughter. Little help he'd been.

This visit would be much longer and he knew it, but the situation was different. This time, lives didn't depend on his return. Far from it. Right now they depended on his absence.

God. He could barely stand thinking about it. Trust had been shattered, and shattered badly.

But now he was here, making a nuisance of himself. He had the distinct, unsurprising feeling that Elaine would be happier if he'd stayed away. What was he if not a reminder of her late husband? Besides, he'd never really gotten to know Elaine. In school she'd been four years behind him; then he'd left for college and his current job. They were damn near strangers.

And Cassie. She might be his niece, but he'd done a lousy job of being her uncle. He'd been a rotten godfather, too. That implied some obligation, as did the blood relationship. What business did he have now of developing a relationship with such a young child, who might not see him again for a year or more? Or even longer?

Damn, he should have gone elsewhere. Anywhere. Somewhere he could be sure of not messing up the lives of his family.

Devlin, without thinking about it, reached for the pack of cigarettes he used to carry in his breast pocket. His flannel-shirt pocket felt empty. Of course. He'd quit ages ago. A habit was harder to get rid of than a physical addiction.

He shook his head a bit, stepping down onto a cracked sidewalk, giving serious thought as to whether he should stay in this house. The motel was an option, one he should at least check out.

Except for his mother. He shook his head again and considered Lu. He knew she'd been annoyed for some time over the fact that he came home so seldom. Hell, to be honest about it, he rarely came home at all. A trip for his brother's wedding? Another for Cassie's baptism? Not a record to be proud of.

Then Caleb had died, which he was sure had just about killed his mom, and he still hadn't come home except for a week for the funeral. A while after he'd returned overseas, she'd emailed him to tell him she was selling the house.

It did her no good, she said, to be rattling around in that big old place by herself. Besides, Elaine and her grand-daughter needed her help.

So here she was. Here *he* was. In the house Caleb had bought for his new family. A house his brother would never share with them.

God!

Just as he'd made up his mind to take his car and head to the motel, his mother pulled up in the driveway. She still drove her aging silver Volvo. It wasn't until Lu climbed out that she saw Devlin.

Her mouth dropped open; then her purse fell to the ground, and she opened her arms and hurried toward him. Devlin met her halfway, lifting her off her feet in a bear hug. Only then did he realize just how much he had missed her.

When he set Lu on her feet, she stepped back, holding his forearms, and said, "Let me get a look at you, boy."

It gave him a chance to look at her as well. The last couple of years had taken some weight off her. Maybe too much? Her hair had turned almost completely gray, and the lines had deepened in her face. Her skin looked soft and smooth, though, as if it had never really aged. Bright hazel eyes looked up at him from above a mouth that had once sung him lullabies and kissed his small hurts.

She was beautiful to him, and always would be.

"How long you here for?" she demanded as her smiling eyes scoped him. "Damn, it's good to see you. But how long? A few days? A week?"

Her small expectation caused a pang in him. "Longer this time," he promised. "Maybe a month or more."

For the second time, Lu's mouth dropped open; then her face creased with concern. "You get fired?"

Under other circumstances, he might have laughed. Shame pricked him as he realized he'd neglected Lu to the point that she thought he must have been fired if he was going to visit for more than a few days.

He shook his head. "I built up too much unused vacation time. The bean counters booted me out the door and told me not to come back until I'd used most of it."

"Smart bean counters," she said, then laughed. "You'll be staying here, of course. We've got a little room."

"Elaine was pretty definite about it."

Lu nodded. "She would be. She's got a good heart. And Cassie. Did you meet Cassie?"

"She's beautiful, but busy with her crayons."

He saw something like sorrow flit over his mother's face, but it swiftly left and her smile returned.

"Well, since you're here, help me with the groceries."

Just like old times, he thought as he rounded the back end of the Volvo and opened the trunk. Help with the groceries. Ever since he was old enough to lift a bag.

Except now the bags were reusable, with handles.

Elaine helped put everything away, the two women chatting companionably. Cassie sat in a chair at the table and simply watched.

He'd heard from his mom some time back that Cassie had some developmental problems, but the subject had been skimmed over as if minor. After watching Cassie color so intently despite his arrival, despite his conversation with Elaine, he wasn't sure it was exactly minor. Especially now, when the child seemed totally focused on the process of putting groceries away. No chatter, no moving around, no attempts to help or curiosity about the items being stored. Just focused observation.

But then, what did he know about young children? Zip.

Once everything was put away, Lu started a fresh pot of coffee. "Now to get Devlin settled," she said briskly.

"The office," Elaine responded. "I'll start moving some things out of the way."

Devlin straightened. "I can help with that."

Elaine shook her head. "There's not much. You'd just get in the way. How about you get your suitcase?"

Passing by, Lu patted his cheek. She had to reach up because he'd outgrown her by nearly a foot. "It really isn't much. Now, go get your things."

A corner of his mouth lifted. She was still his mother and acting as if he were still ten. He kinda liked it, actually. It had been so many years—maybe too many. A grown man, he stood on his own two feet and leaned on no one. He also had no one to care for him in the small, important ways.

"Okay," he said, and turned to go out to his car. He'd started to think he should cut this visit short, to maybe a week or so, and go to another town, a place where he wouldn't be creating a tidal wave of complications for these two women.

Then he realized he was trying to slip into an old habit, one that had made him a stranger to his own mother. Move on and move along, and make no deep emotional connections no matter where he landed. He couldn't afford to care deeply.

Except he already had an emotional connection here,

and he couldn't leave yet. Not when his mother kept looking at him and getting a huge smile on her face.

Move along? No, not yet.

FROM HALF A world away, two people had come looking for him, trying painstakingly to follow his travels. To find out where he'd gone and where he remained.

The search might have been more difficult except they had contacts of their own. When fairly certain they had been given most of the information they needed, travel became their primary goal. Their primary purpose.

They couldn't wait too long, or their target might move again. The way he'd been moving for weeks now.

The desire for vengeance drove them. It was a hungry master.

They ignored everything else.

Chapter Three

Elaine headed to work three days later, thinking Devlin's visit wasn't as much of an imposition as she'd almost feared. As houseguests went, he ought to get a gold star. No messes or forgotten dishes anywhere so far. Everything he'd brought with him tucked away neatly in her office. Even last evening, he'd made himself nearly invisible.

It was almost as if he wasn't there, except for when he sat with Lu and carried on a mostly one-sided conversation. If Devlin had much to say about his life, Elaine doubted she'd ever hear it.

Cassie had begun to relax around him, too, to judge by breakfast this morning, although she wasn't yet interested in making him part of her life. She watched but didn't talk. Lu let her be while still trying to make sure she felt like part of it all.

Lu, Elaine often thought, was amazing, an angel.

At her work office, however, her thoughts did a quick one-eighty turn. Bixby, the rancher, was a big part of the conversation still.

Detective Guy Redwing, along with deputies Connie Parish and Kerri Canaday, filled her in.

"Bixby wasn't kidding about those trespassers, Elaine," Connie said. "They were camping out there on the Sel-

vage side of the fence. I'd guess the Selvages haven't noticed yet."

Elaine plopped down in one of the office chairs. She'd
wondered, in some small, unkind part of her brain, whether
Bixby had been exaggerating. Evidently not. "Seriously?
How many?"

Guy shrugged. "Maybe six or seven that we saw. Anyway, we moved them out yesterday afternoon. Gave them
a trespass warning, including the part about how the landowners might shoot them on sight. They left."

"They'll be back," Kerri remarked, stroking the white
fur of her service dog, Snowy. "Nothing they said made
it sound otherwise."

Guy shook his head. "Damn fools. And all because
there's some lights in the sky. Could be almost anything."

"You'd think," Elaine said. "I saw them when I was out
there. I got a real scare thinking they might be part of a
range fire, but Bixby told me he's been seeing them most
of his life and they don't hurt anything."

Kerri cocked a brow at her. "So you saw them, too?"

"They were what made me pull into Bixby's place. I
thought, like I said, I was seeing a range fire. Damn radios and phones wouldn't work, though."

Connie snorted. "Typical. They almost never do out
there."

No news there, Elaine thought. "Well, I guess we'll have
to keep an eye on this before someone gets shot. Bixby
was sure ready when I was out there. Waving his shotgun,
spittle flying."

"You can't blame him," Connie said. "It's hard enough
making money off a ranch these days without fools in-
terfering. Ethan, my husband, is working Micah's sheep
ranch with him. Well, you guys know that. All I was

gonna say was, wool isn't doing much better than beef, either."

Elaine nodded. She glanced over at the coffee urn and saw Velma, the dispatcher who must be at least half as old as the county, sitting at her console and puffing on a cigarette below the *No Smoking* sign that was tacked to the wall. That was Velma—she'd been the department's dispatcher for as long as anyone could remember, and no one was going to fire her. Nobody even thought about it.

But Velma's presence meant Velma had made the coffee in the big urn. The bottles of various antacids that lined the coffee bar attested to the quality of the brew. Which meant that if Elaine wanted coffee she could enjoy, she needed to take her thermos across the way to Maude's diner.

She could have laughed, but then she'd have to explain why. Nope. Not in Velma's hearing. She turned her attention back to Connie, Guy and Kerri. "I guess I should stop and talk with the Selvages on my patrol today. Unless you did yesterday?"

Guy shook his head. "The loonies were still gone after we scared 'em off the day before. Can't prove they'll be back. So what could I say to Lew? Hell, for all I know, Lew Selvage won't care. He's got a much bigger spread than Bixby. Healthier, too."

Elaine blew out a long breath that briefly puffed her cheeks. "Okay, I'll stop and talk to Lew. He's got hired hands he needs to warn. I hope we can get through this without any corpses."

Connie shook her head. "You know I'm not bloodthirsty, but you gotta wonder about people who think they have a right to run all over private land."

"Without getting hurt," Elaine added. "Like it or not, it's the same as breaking into someone's house."

"Well, not quite," Kerri said dryly, making Elaine laugh.

She picked up her thermos, then headed down a few doors across from Main Street and entered Maude's diner. It was properly known as the City Café, but Elaine didn't think she'd heard anyone call it that in her entire life.

It was not a large diner, more of a cozy place, but large enough to be a breakfast gathering spot for a lot of retired older men, and later for a lunch hour for workers in the surrounding shops. The diner never lacked for customers.

This morning, however, the place felt strange. Elaine reached the counter and found herself facing Mavis, Maude's daughter, a virtual clone of her blunt and stocky mother.

Mavis took Elaine's insulated bottle without asking; it was a morning ritual. Then Elaine scanned the dining area and saw a few faces she didn't recognize.

When Mavis handed back the thermos, Elaine remarked, "Got some tourists, huh?"

Mavis snorted. "Don't know what they are. Sure ain't here for hunting or hiking. More like weirdos. But they ain't talking to me." She gave a harsh laugh. "Not sure I wanna hear nothing from them anyways."

Now Elaine's curiosity nagged full strength. She picked up her bottle, then headed toward the table with the four men and one woman she didn't recognize. The advantage of being a sheriff's deputy was that she could ask casual questions of strangers.

Before she reached the table, five sets of eyes turned her way. They knew she was headed for them, and swiftly exchanged looks. Something to hide?

"Howdy," she said pleasantly, putting a smile on her face. "You folks visiting us for a while?"

Looks were exchanged again. Then, silently, they appeared to have decided on a mouthpiece. The woman, with long dark hair caught in a ponytail, a woman who didn't look as if she'd even reached her midtwenties, spoke.

"Just a while," she answered.

"And you are?"

The woman's chin thrust forward a bit, as if she resented being questioned, but she didn't hesitate and didn't seem to have anything to hide. "I'm Lotte Berg. Who are you?"

Elaine's smile broadened. A young woman with spunk—she always liked seeing that. "I'm Deputy Elaine Paltier." She pointed to the embroidery on the front of her jacket. "And here's my badge number, if you feel like complaining because I asked for your name."

The entire group recoiled slightly at that, even the brave Lotte Berg. Apparently they didn't want that kind of encounter with a cop.

Elaine leaned back against the edge of a nearby booth. "We don't see many new faces around here. We get curious. So are you here for hunting? Wrong season, I'm afraid—but that would be true most places. Hiking?"

Now Lotte looked irritated. "We haven't done anything wrong, so it's none of your business."

One of the guys drew a sharp breath. Elaine set her bottle on the table in the booth behind her, pulled out an empty chair at the table where the group had gathered and sat with them.

"Well," she said slowly, looking at each face in turn, "it might could be my business. You go hiking up in the mountains or camping... Do you have any idea how fast the weather changes up there? We can get snow in July. Then there's rain. We're talking hypothermia here."

"So?" Lotte demanded.

"So you could die. You have any way of calling for help if somebody breaks an ankle? Or if you get lost? Cell phones don't work too good in the mountains. Any of you got a satellite phone? Regardless, it'd be wise to tell the forest service ranger where you want to hike and when you expect to be back."

Blank looks greeted her. Which told her instantly that these kids weren't at all familiar with the mountains. Great. Maybe it would be best if they bothered Lew Selvage after all.

Lotte suddenly looked a bit sullen. "We're not going into the mountains."

"Good," Elaine said amiably, getting ready to stand. "We don't like having to send out rescue parties for people who should know better." She paused. "If not the mountains, then what?"

No one answered. Looks passed around again.

Elaine stood, twisting a bit to grab her bottle. Then she looked down at them once more. "I don't know where you're from. But be careful of trespassing in these parts. You might find yourselves evicted at the end of a rifle or shotgun."

As she left, Mavis gave her a nod of approval. Elaine didn't feel she deserved it. She'd done what she could but figured it wasn't enough.

Driving out to the Selvage property gave her plenty of time to think. She scanned the roads, of course, looking for any kind of trouble. She laughed to herself. Trouble out here was likely to be a calf that had found its way past a fence and wandering in the road. Or a downed fence that created the possibility of a bigger problem.

Inevitably, her thoughts turned to Devlin. He really *was* a good houseguest. Yesterday—her second unexpected day off, brought about by the sheriff saying she looked tired—Devlin had limited himself to chatting with his mother and occasionally her. He'd even been respectful of Cassie's choice to be left alone. Unlike many people, he didn't press her to talk to him, or help himself to some of her crayons to prove he was a good guy who could color with her.

Elaine treasured her days off. She didn't have to "be on" for other people. No expectations, no duties—just time to be with Cassie. And with Lu, when her mother-in-law didn't take off to spend an afternoon with her friends.

Lu needed the breaks, too. Cassie wasn't troublesome, but she created a problem for those who loved her. Everyone wanted to help, but there seemed to be no way to open Cassie's world. She chose the people she would let in, the activities she preferred, and ignored the rest.

Elaine often tried not to think about the problems Cassie faced, because whenever she did, she grew so sad she wanted to cry.

So, for now, she dragged her thoughts away from Cassie and Devlin to wondering how Lew Selvage would react to all this. UFO hunters. For God's sake.

She knew people saw lights in the sky in the wide-open and scarcely occupied places out there, but most were shrugged off. Ranchers and farmers had more important issues to think about than wondering about some light, even though it might grow large. Elaine was sure most of these sightings were never mentioned or talked about.

Who'd want his neighbors to think he was crazy? It

was like Beggan Bixby. Those red lights had been there most of his life, and they didn't bother anything so he didn't worry about them.

What he was worried about were the trespassers—justifiably so.

Five of them in Maude's this morning. Were they the only ones? Were more coming?

"Ah, crap," she said to the interior of her vehicle. Five, maybe eight, could be handled; more than a dozen could become a serious problem. Larger groups were apt to be more defiant of land boundaries and a few cops.

Someone was going to get hurt. Maybe killed. And she didn't know what to do other than warn the UFO guys off.

At last the entrance to the Selvage ranch appeared to the right. Another mile and she'd be at the house. If Lew wasn't there, she'd have to call him on the sat phone, which wasn't going to make him happy if he was out on the range doing something.

Oh, well. He deserved a warning.

Lew *was* there, however. He came out onto his large porch to greet her as she approached. A short man, he was whipcord lean from a lot of hard work and owned a weathered face from years on the range. Anybody who thought raising cattle meant sitting on your duff until the time arrived to sell them at market ought to come out and try working with Lew or any other rancher.

He wore the standard uniform of jeans—nearly worn white in places—and a checked Western shirt beneath a shearling vest. He touched the brim of his black hat in greeting as she climbed out of her Suburban.

"Hey, what's up, Deputy?" he asked. "Don't recall having any problems."

Elaine shook her head as she approached, then shook

his calloused hand. "You may have one already. I'm not sure, but I know Mr. Bixby has a trespasser problem. We've warned them off, but I'm frankly not sure they'll stay away."

Lew waved her over to a wooden rocker. "I'll get us some coffee, then you can tell me about this gang."

Gang? Elaine didn't want anyone thinking of them that way. A desire to drive them off was one thing, but feeling free to shoot people who had been designated as criminals in many minds wouldn't be good at all.

Lew returned with two mugs and handed her one before settling in the other rocker. "So what's up with these trespassers that's got Bixby so mad? I swear, that man can explode about anything."

Remembering how Beggan Bixby had danced around with that shotgun and spat while ranting to her, Elaine privately agreed. "Well, he was angry, all right. Justifiably so, it seems. He's got those red lights. You've seen them?"

"Hell yeah. From one corner of my ranch. I don't like the way them damn things move around. But near as I can tell, they ain't doing any harm. Bixby's been seeing them for years. So what's the problem?"

Elaine couldn't quite suppress a grimace. "A bunch of people who think they're UFOs. Bothering Bixby's cattle. I don't know yet if they've crossed his fence, but he seems to think so." She tucked away the news that those lights moved around. As if that would help anything.

"Oh, hell," Lew said. He put his cup on a small wooden table between the two rockers. "That'd get him wound up. It'd get me wound up, too. I guess I need to have my ranch hands check the fence along Bixby's land. If someone has been cutting it…" He let the sentence trail off.

But Elaine didn't need him to finish it. She drained her

mug and stood. "Lew, you don't need me to tell you that you don't want the crime scene team all over your land because some idiot got shot."

Lew offered a crooked smile. "Trespassing," he said.

"I get it." Elaine shook her head and sighed. "But there would still have to be an investigation, trespassers or not, stand your ground or not."

She waved to him as she drove away, wondering where all this would lead.

No way to know.

DEVLIN TOOK THE afternoon to wander around Conard City. Some things had changed, he noticed, but not very many since he'd lived here the first couple decades of his life.

The school appeared to be the same except for a larger sports field. The hospital was bigger. The community college was probably the biggest change of all, as was a group of apartment buildings that seemed to be acting mostly as student housing. The park's trees and flowers had clearly become lusher with time. Familiar, yet a little unfamiliar.

He learned most about the changes from pausing to chat with people, some of whom remembered him. By and large, though, no one seemed reluctant to talk about the town.

He was a little annoyed he hadn't taken the time to walk around when he was here for his brother's funeral, renew some acquaintances. But then, he acknowledged, this no longer felt like home to him. Or like his hometown.

His job had taken him into a wider, different world. One that had changed him irrevocably. One that had moved him so far from Conard City and Conard County that he doubted either would ever feel like home again.

Honestly, though, he hadn't come back to this particular place to revive memories. He'd come to see his mother. To see his godchild, his niece. He'd been too absent to be a real uncle to the little girl. He even felt ashamed, knowing that Caleb would have expected better of him. Would have had every right to.

But his job hadn't given him a whole lot of leeway.

And that job had apparently caused someone to die. This had seemed like the safest place to come, his connections here so tenuous. A place to stay out of the way while his contacts were protected.

But the town seemed to have grown a whole new batch of strangers, from what little Elaine had said.

Knowing how little change this town was used to, a snort of laughter escaped him, drawing looks from passing pedestrians. He gave them a smile and a wave and kept walking.

Maude's, he decided. Instead of letting Lu cook yet again. He pulled his cell phone out of his pocket and called her. She sounded only too glad to have fried chicken, potato salad and fruit for dinner.

"Cassie loves fried chicken," Lu said.

"Well, I hope you do, too."

His mother laughed. "Of course I do. And Maude makes the best."

So he headed to Maude's, his personal list growing to include a pie. A peach pie. *Oh, yeah.*

Then he found himself facing Sheriff Gage Dalton on the sidewalk near Maude's. Gage looked pleasant enough—at least as pleasant as he could with half his face covered by a burn scar. A man who would forever limp because of a bomb that had killed his first family. A man who lived with constant pain.

Devlin remembered him from his youth here, back

when Gage had been known as Hell's Own Archangel as he walked off the agony of his losses at night on the streets of this small town. A face without expression, eyes black as midnight.

The man had changed over the years. He offered Devlin a half smile, the most his face could do anymore. "Nice to see you again."

"It's been a while," Devlin agreed. He wondered if he was about to get the third degree, considering how rarely he'd been in this town and how short his visits had been. A wedding and a funeral? Sounded like a bad joke.

"Staying a while?"

Devlin cracked his own smile, covering the darker thoughts that had haunted him for years. "About a month. Blame it on the bean counters. Apparently they don't want to pay me for unused vacation.".

Gage lifted a brow. "But no other vacations in all these years?"

Devlin realized he'd walked into a trap he needed to ease his way out of. *All these years?* The subtler way of asking why he hadn't come back here much. Good question.

One he couldn't truthfully answer. But even while on vacation, he still needed to protect the people who worked for him, all of them out there in dangerous places, in danger of losing their lives if anyone found out their relationship with Devlin. That need usually didn't carry him far from headquarters, but this time, someone had died. He fought that memory back into the black box in his mind. "I'm a workaholic," he replied to Dalton. "The policy on vacations just changed."

Gage nodded, clearly only partially convinced.

Well, hell, what was he supposed to do about that? His life was already a mess of lies, and now he needed to add another. No, he decided. He would not. If Gage wanted to check him out, he'd get the official unshakable cover story. At least he and his colleagues thought it was unshakable.

Gage spoke after a few moments of studying him. "Enjoy your stay," he said and headed for the diner.

A second of indecision, then Devlin fell in beside him. "I told my mother I'd bring home some of Maude's fried chicken for dinner."

Gage smiled. "Best damn chicken I ever tasted. What about you? Being overseas all these years must have given you a taste for exotic foods."

Devlin had to laugh. "Sure, when I get out of the embassy. But our cafeteria makes a mean burger, too."

It was Gage's turn to laugh. "Hadn't thought about that."

Inside the diner, they parted ways, Gage heading over to a table to chat, Devlin going to the counter to order dinner.

When he stepped outside again, he felt uneasy. Looking around quickly, he saw nothing out of the ordinary, but the feeling didn't dissipate.

Hell. Once he rounded the corner, the sensation disappeared. He shook his head a little. Had he become paranoid because of that incident in Chechnya? Maybe so.

Another thing to work on. He seemed to have developed plenty of self-improvement projects over the years.

State Department. Ha!

Chapter Four

In the early evening, about to finish her shift, Elaine swung by the Bixby ranch. She could at least find out if there had been any more trouble since her fellow deputies had warned off the nuts.

It ought to make those trespassers more than a little uneasy that so many cops had an eye on them. Or that shooting them would be legal. Well, *might* be legal, although she wasn't about to tell those UFO guys it might not be. It was enough to let the ranchers know there'd be complications, an investigation regardless of their reasons. Nobody needed that.

Beggan Bixby was sitting on his front porch. His shotgun wasn't far away.

"Hey," Elaine said as she approached. "Still having trouble?"

"Not since those deputies came out here. Went out to check for myself."

She nodded, standing at the foot of the three steps that climbed to his porch. "So maybe it's settled."

Bixby snorted. "Like hell."

Elaine placed one hand on her hip, the side away from her holster. She'd been hoping that the peace, however temporary, would have calmed Bixby. Apparently it had not.

"Mr. Bixby, it's legally questionable if you shoot those trespassers."

"They're on my land!"

"You'd still wind up in the middle of a murder investigation. Maybe even wind up in court. You don't really need me to tell you that. But what good would it do your herd?"

That seemed to deprive him of speech. Finally, he said, "I can shoot trespassers. It's the *law*."

"Yup," she agreed. "Except a court is going to have to figure out the fine details of that law. Drive 'em off, but don't do it by pulling a trigger."

She left him with his mouth hanging open. Hardly surprising. A lot of folks thought they had rights they didn't. Like shooting people.

Well, she sure didn't like the way this might go. Lew Selvage, she trusted to be reasonable and deal with the problem in a way that wouldn't get him tangled up in some kind of legal mess. Bixby's fury might override any common sense he had.

She thought of those people she had warned at Maude's and decided she'd have to check tomorrow to see if they'd left town. Or if any more were arriving.

Because now that the Bixby spread was on the "UFO map," other seekers would probably show up, even for just a couple of red lights. Man!

When she got home, she was greeted by the mouthwatering aroma of fried chicken. Maude's. Nothing smelled quite like it.

Cassie emerged from the kitchen with a genuine smile. She wore her favorite outfit, pink leggings and a pink T-shirt with a sparkly butterfly on it. "Mommy," she said.

. The sound of the word melted Elaine's heart. Cassie had started saying it only a month or so ago.

Elaine squatted, hoping against hope that Cassie would come to her for a hug. It didn't happen. It might never happen.

Instead, Cassie turned and went back to the kitchen.

"Food," she said.

Well, food was always a good thing. Especially when it smelled like that.

In short order, the four of them sat at the table with full plates.

WHILE EVERYONE TUCKED in and Elaine thanked Devlin for bringing dinner, he was looking at Cassie, thinking for the first time how hard this might be for his niece. Thinking for the first time that Caleb should be here to help her.

Like it had been Caleb's choice. He turned his thoughts away from that. He didn't need the guilt trip that was on the menu every time he thought of his brother and his brother's family. At least Elaine had Lu to help her. Even if Caleb's big brother was proving useless.

"How did your day go?" he asked Elaine.

"It was interesting, that's for sure." Her mouth tipped into a faint smile. "Nothing like UFOs to add a little excitement."

"UFOs? Really?"

Lu spoke. "Now this I wanna hear."

No reason to keep it secret. Protecting Beggan Bixby's privacy had probably long since gone by the wayside, given the speed of the local grapevine. Given the fact that, in his state of mind, Bixby had probably complained to everyone he knew. And why not?

The worst of it was, Elaine was sure he was probably

blaming the sheriff's department more than the invaders. Those complaints might give Gage Dalton trouble in the next election.

"Dang," she murmured to herself. This was hardly a political issue and, regardless, she was supposed to be worrying about the law, not the politics.

"What?" asked Lu.

"I just thought about how the politics of this whole situation might give Gage some trouble in the next election."

Lu snorted. "This county loves that man. Anyway, nobody's ever tried to stand against him. And what brought that on?"

"Beggan Bixby. UFOs. UFO hunters, I think they call themselves. And five or more strangers trespassing on Bixby's ranch to look at two red lights." She tilted her head. "I talked to five of them at Maude's, but I'm not sure they're the only ones going out at night to hunt those lights." She shook her head, thinking more detective work might be required, and returned her attention to the fried chicken.

Lu spoke, raising her eyebrows. "As often as those lights show up? God knows what they are, but is that worth traipsing out over rangeland in the middle of the night to take pictures?"

Elaine glanced at Devlin to find him smiling. Man, did he have a gorgeous smile. The kind that made a woman's heart skip a time or two.

"There are lots of believers," he said. "And judging by recent information, some of those UAPs can't be identified. Or brushed aside."

Elaine nodded. "You're right. Even so, now we have people driving Beggan Bixby crazy. They're trespassing and disturbing his cattle. Not a good thing when you consider how nervous cattle don't fatten as well."

"I didn't know that," Devlin remarked.

"You aren't here enough to know about such things," his mother answered tartly.

Elaine didn't miss the way Devlin looked down. Just briefly, just enough for her to realize that stung. So when it came to his mother, he could still feel scolded. That amused her but also made her like him more. The man who rarely revealed anything about himself, at least not during his brief visits, had just revealed quite a bit.

"So," he asked, "what can you do about these UFO hunters? If they're upsetting Bixby, then they should get off his land, right?"

"Exactly," Elaine said. "We warned them off. Unless they've left town, they'll be back out there soon. I need to check if they're still here. Or if more of them have come."

Lu spoke. "I can't believe all this fuss over a couple of red lights. Sure, they're weird, but who knows?"

"I haven't seen them before," Elaine said. "The other night, they were so big and orange I thought we had a range fire."

"Well, that's new," Lu answered before picking up a drumstick. "They were never that big when I saw them. Always thought they were lights on a tower or something."

"Well, they were big enough that I was in a real hurry to get the firefighters out there. Except, of course, my radio, cell and sat phone weren't working."

She shrugged.

Lu chuckled. "Never fails when you need 'em most."

"Anyway, Bixby was fit to be tied, mad at us because we haven't gotten rid of the trespassers and he pays taxes, too. Oh yeah, then there was the shotgun."

At that, Lu drew a sharp breath. "Elaine…"

"I wasn't really worried about him shooting me, Lu. He wanted to shoot some other people."

"Still…" Lu shook her head. "Your job isn't usually dangerous."

Elaine kept her lips sealed. She always tried to make it all seem safe for Lu and Cassie's sake, but it wasn't always. No cop's job could always be without threat.

Elaine looked at her daughter and saw she was picking at her food. Evidently, Cassie had eaten enough. "Time for a bath, Cassie?"

Cassie shook her head. "No!"

Another word her child had learned. Elaine stared at her, knowing they came to this sometimes, knowing it would only cause Cassie to totally withdraw if she pressed the issue. Or worse, cause a serious meltdown.

"Okay," she said after a moment. "We have to wash your hands and face, though. Greasy from the chicken." And everything else Cassie had eaten with her fingers.

After a few seconds, Cassie nodded. She'd tolerate the touching for that long.

DEVLIN WATCHED ELAINE coax Cassie to the bathroom, then helped Lu clean up the dinner mess. They chatted casually, and at some point, Devlin realized a gulf had grown between them over the years. This was not the kind of easy chatting that occurred between people who were close. They were two strangers working their way to some kind of relationship. It was a state he was familiar with in his job but uncomfortable with his own mother.

God, he'd been away too long.

Later, as night took over the world, he stepped outside

and stood in the near dark, arms folded and legs apart. He once again felt uneasy, as if the night held a threat.

It well might, he supposed. Intelligence sometimes had holes in it.

His bosses pretty much dismissed it, knowing the real threat was for Devlin's contacts overseas. And they were right. With a war going on over there, nobody would look for him any farther than the other side of the town.

But there was always a risk he might inadvertently reveal something that would give away another of his contacts.

So he'd come here, the most out-of-the-way place in his life. There was nothing he could do here that would expose anyone.

But the threat he felt was inchoate yet. It seemed to seep through the night with no focus. He'd felt that before in foreign lands, but his job always brought some danger with it. Always. This was different.

Just paranoia, he told himself. A learned response to constantly being a stranger in a strange land. Even here.

But it wasn't often that he suspected he might be a direct target. He thrust the paranoia onto a back burner but refused to douse it entirely. Fear, remaining alert, had been useful his entire adult life.

CONARD CITY WAS a small town. Not as small as some towns the foreign women were used to, but small enough that strangers might be noticed. They carefully stayed to the edges, watching the daily lives of the townspeople, trying to ascertain rhythms. To figure out under what circumstances they could risk being seen without being noticed.

To figure out how to pick out one man from the many,

a man whose face they didn't even know. A man whose name had never been given to them. The people who had sent them here either didn't know—which wouldn't be surprising when dealing with a spy—or didn't want them to know because it might reveal a secret.

Either way, the women weren't happy with any of it.

That would require talking to people, a dangerous thing to do when you only had questions that might arouse suspicions. When you had a foreign accent and a questionable command of English.

Maybe the man they wanted to find was a stranger here, too? Might he already stood out? But how would they tell the difference?

They found a spot in the woods near a trickling stream and made a rugged camp for themselves. Life had taught them to make do: a tent from their outer cloaks. Foraging for most of their food. Snaring a rabbit.

The number of animals surprised them. War, they surmised, hadn't decimated the wildlife here the way it had at home. But then, nothing around here had been turned into rubble by endless conflict.

Hunkering down, they tried to plan, only to realize that their original plan, the one that had brought them halfway around the world, had been incomplete. But how could it have been any better when they had no way of knowing what they might find once they arrived?

They ought to be pleased they had gotten this far, which was no mean task. It had taken a contact at their *own* consulate to point them this way. To arm them with a gun and poison. To tell them this much. They'd been fortunate in that because the woman had sympathized with their mission, hadn't demanded some form of bribe the way most men would have.

But she hadn't been able to identify the man they sought in any meaningful way. Evidently he hid behind a wall of secrets.

They'd also developed an uneasy appreciation for how much one side knew about the other. How could their consulate know where this man had gone to hide? Come to that, how could they know about this faceless, nameless monster at all?

Because of someone like their brother, someone who had been spying on this man? Perhaps someone who had betrayed their brother and not the American at all.

The awareness gave them shivers. This was a world they didn't know. They were used to an obvious war, actions in the open for the most part. Not secrets behind closed doors.

It also gave them plenty to wonder about. As they sat shivering around a tiny fire and the wind from the mountains blew an icy breath from the glaciers above, they had plenty to talk about and worry about.

Their brother had been betrayed. The man who had recruited Niko was responsible for his death; he must have somehow let it be known that Niko was informing. Directly or indirectly didn't matter.

That, they figured out without any trouble. But the woman at the consulate in Los Angeles gave them more reasons to fear. She had known where the American man had gone. How had she known? And now she knew that Zoe and Kalina had come after him. How could she be trusted not to reveal that to the people in the American Embassy that she must have talked to just to get this little bit of information?

The young women sat shivering, and their fear slowly deepened until it became almost as strong as their thirst for vengeance. Niko might not be the last one to be betrayed.

Miserably they realized they might have made some huge mistakes. They should run now. Right now.

But they refused to give up on their need for vengeance. They'd known from the start they could be killed.

They just hadn't suspected death might come from someone they had trusted.

And they still had to find a way to get into that town, to collect information without being obvious.

They'd never dreamed they would ever be aimed at like a bullet at a target.

THE NEXT DAY brought a powdering of snow, not unheard of even as the trees leafed out for the spring. The white dusting didn't last past the noonday sun, though, but the air remained invigoratingly crisp.

Lu insisted on making breakfast for the four of them even though Devlin offered to pick up food at Maude's or the truck stop.

"Don't deprive me," she said to Devlin. "For years and years, I enjoyed making breakfast for your dad. His favorite meal of the day."

Soon bacon sizzled in a large frying pan, eggs were beaten with a bit of milk and slices of bread were toasted and buttered. And Lu wanted no help, not even from Elaine.

Elaine's curiosity had been carefully tamped for days now, but it refused to be silenced permanently. She eyed Devlin over her coffee. "So what exactly do you do for the State Department?"

"A little of this and that."

She snorted. *"Right."* She drew the word out.

He laughed. "Yeah. I'm a foreign service officer. Depending on where I'm posted, I may be a diplomatic attaché."

"So more than one hat?"

He nodded, admiring the plate of food Lu placed in front of him. "Mom, that looks fabulous!"

"Told you I'm good at making breakfast. You ought to remember." She placed another plate in front of Elaine, then a small one in front of Cassie.

Cassie regarded her food with some interest, then pointed to the scrambled eggs. "Yellow." Another one of Cassie's very few words. The names of colors seemed to attract her, though.

Elaine braced herself. This might go badly. "Yes, the eggs are yellow."

Cassie shoved them off her plate and onto the table. Then she picked up a strip of bacon and began to eat.

Lu ignored the mess and sat with her own plate across from Elaine. "Oh, these yellow eggs are yummy," she said as she lifted a forkful.

"They sure are," Elaine replied, helping herself to her own. "I love yellow eggs."

No response from Cassie, who seemed quite content with bacon and toast.

After a minute, Elaine spoke again. "These yellow eggs are so good. Do you want to try just a little bit, Cassie?"

Cassie looked up from her bacon at the pile of scrambled eggs by the edge of her plate, which by now had to be cold. Not good. But still…

Elaine ate another mouthful of eggs, pretending to ignore Cassie, leaving her alone like she wanted.

But, causing Elaine's heart to leap, Cassie finally reached out a thumb and finger and pinched the tiniest bit of egg and carried it to her mouth.

Elaine reacted immediately with positive reinforcement. "That was so brave of you, Cassie, to try the yellow eggs! I'm proud of you!"

Then she let it go.

DEVLIN, WATCHING ALL THIS, felt a strong pang for Elaine. Over the last few days, he'd gotten a much clearer idea of all she and her daughter were dealing with, and it definitely looked like an awful situation for Elaine.

He could see the pain in her eyes when she reached out in some way to Cassie and she didn't respond. He could read the yearning on her face for just one little hug or touch.

He couldn't imagine how hard that had to be for Elaine. Yet she always remained calm and patient with Cassie. Always warm.

So did his mother. In just brief flashes, Lu was more like a protective tiger, though. Protective of Cassie. Devlin wondered if Elaine showed that side, too, sometimes. Probably.

Guilt speared him. What if he had quit his job and stayed here to look after Cassie and Elaine after Caleb died? Yet, looking at Cassie now, he wondered how he could have made a difference. If Cassie wasn't connecting with her mother in any deep emotional way, why would she have connected with him?

He closed his eyes briefly, squashing a guilt that bordered on the self-aggrandizing. No reason to think he'd have had any more impact than anyone else.

Lu started clearing the table. Cassie's plate was mostly empty of bacon and toast, but the eggs still lay on the table. Most of them, anyway.

Cassie slid off her chair and got her crayons and coloring book from the counter. Lu moved quickly to clear away the eggs before anything landed on them.

Then Cassie started coloring her unicorn while her mom looked on sadly.

God, Devlin thought. Yet somehow sorrow didn't hang over this house. It didn't dog these two women's every waking moment, every step. They were remarkable.

"Sally's coming today, right?" Elaine asked.

"At eleven," his mother answered.

"Sally?" Devlin asked.

Elaine gave him a small smile. "Sally's helping Cassie. Right, Cassie?"

Cassie shrugged.

"Her support therapist," Elaine elaborated. "She helps all of us."

"But not today," Lu reminded her. "Today is Cassie's alone."

"That's right."

Lu tilted her head. "So find a reason to get out of here. Since you're not in uniform, I guess you have the day off. Go have a chilly picnic or something."

"That sounds like a great idea," Devlin said, rising, his determination growing. Elaine needed time that wasn't filled every single second with her job and Cassie. *Well, I ought to know something about that,* he thought wryly. He wasn't good at taking time for himself, either. "I wouldn't mind familiarizing myself with the area. I've been away so long I feel like a stranger." He looked at Elaine. "At least, if you don't mind the company."

Now she tilted her head back, looking up at him. "Sounds okay to me," she said after a barely perceptible hesitation.

So maybe okay, he thought. Fair enough.

Elaine told Cassie where she was going and offered her

an invitation to join them for the picnic. Cassie clearly wasn't interested, so Elaine slid off her chair, promising to return soon. Cassie remained superficially indifferent.

A trip to Maude's provided lunch and bottled water. Jackets on, the two headed out into the countryside in Elaine's official vehicle. It seemed, Devlin thought, that she was expected to use it all the time. Just as it seemed she had to strap on her pistol every time she stepped out her front door, even when in civvies, like now.

As the town dropped away behind them and the range began to spread openly over the rolling hills, he asked her about it.

"Are you on duty all the time?"

She glanced at him. "Why?"

"Because you're in your official vehicle and you're wearing your sidearm."

She laughed quietly. "Well…it creates a presence, and we're a small department. Add to that, that everyone around here is armed. Although you see little enough of it in town, it's not wise for a cop to ever be unarmed. We could need it at any moment—not that it happens often."

"I hope not. I don't remember this being the Wild West."

She laughed again. "Civilization arrived a long time ago. We're not having shoot-outs on Main Street."

Which wasn't true of a lot of the places where Devlin had been stationed over the years. He'd become used to an amazing level of violence and doubted anything in Conard County could hold a candle to any of his assignments.

He turned his attention to the passing countryside, trying to touch the boy and young man he'd been so long ago, the one who had grown up here, safer than he'd realized until much later.

"Whoa," Elaine said abruptly.

He looked forward and saw a small knot of people and three cars jammed onto the shoulder. The people appeared to be talking with one another.

"Campers," Elaine said. "Probably our UFO hunters."

Since she wasn't on duty, Devlin expected her to drive by, but instead she slowed to a stop. The group at the roadside had a variety of reactions and were quickly joined by four more.

"More of them have come," Elaine remarked. "I was afraid of that."

She put her vehicle in Park and climbed out. Devlin waited, reluctant to shove himself onto her turf. She didn't need *his* help to handle this. It was her job, after all. But he still itched to get involved and was glad she'd left her window half-open so he could at least hear.

"Howdy," she said, sounding friendly. "You folks doing all right?"

"We're just camping here," said one young man, who sounded more truculent than he probably should have. A greeting to anyone shouldn't sound like you were ready to start a fight, and certainly not with a cop.

Immediately, a young woman inserted herself between Elaine and the young man. *Smart,* Devlin thought.

"Honest," the woman said with a smile. "This is a public campsite, isn't it?"

Elaine nodded. "It sure is. There are turnouts in a lot of isolated places for just this very thing."

The young woman nodded. "I'm Doreen, by the way. This is Alex. We're probably responsible for making the locals crazy. Coming out here to see those lights was our idea."

"And now?"

Doreen raised her hands, open palmed. "We can see some of those lights from here. No problem for anyone, right?"

"Depends on where you watch from and what you're hoping to see. You think there's anything but those lights out there?"

"How would we know?" Doreen answered. "Just the lights are enough right now. Why don't you and your friend come and have some coffee with us? The fire's just back there."

"Thanks, but we're on our way down the road," Elaine said. "But what has you guys so fascinated out here? Just those couple of lights?" Elaine sounded as if she didn't quite believe it, but she kept that suggestion faint, easy not to hear.

"It's more than that," Alex answered, sounding less defensive. "Most people don't want to hear it, though."

"I would," Elaine countered. "Another time?"

"Sure," Doreen said brightly. "Some of us come into that café in town a couple of times a week. Tuesday?"

"Absolutely," Elaine agreed. "I'll see you then."

When she returned to the car and pulled away, Devlin remarked, "They seem inoffensive enough."

"So far. Especially if they stay off private land."

"I can see that." The temperature seemed to be dropping, so he rolled up his window. "So all of this is about some lights?"

"Evidently so. At least as far as I know. I'd like to hear what else they have to say about it."

"Then we should have stayed."

Elaine shook her head. "Before I talk to them again, I want to be sure they haven't gone back to trespassing."

"They've been warned off, haven't they? I don't get

why they'd go back." Not that he wasn't accustomed to people doing things they shouldn't. Part of his job.

"Me, neither, but there's a lot of things I don't get. I suppose I ought to do some research on UFO hunters."

He snorted. "That could get interesting."

"Yeah, and they probably come in more varieties than ice cream."

"Probably. What would you do if they say they've been abducted?"

Elaine let out a full-throated laugh. "Tell 'em aliens aren't in my jurisdiction."

ON THE WAY, although Elaine didn't figure they had a particular destination, she stopped at the Bixby spread. Bixby had rounded up most of his herd into a smaller area, apparently ready for a move.

"Gonna take 'em up to summer pasture," he remarked, punctuating his words with another spit of tobacco on the ground.

"Summer pasture?" Devlin asked.

Bixby eyed him. "Guess you're a greenhorn."

"These days," he admitted.

Bixby nodded, resettling his worn hat on his head. "Cattle need fattening. Land here's kinda dry. So we lease land up in the mountains where there's plenty of good grazing. Get 'em plumped up before selling 'em. Make sure the cows are fit to breed. Problem is, they don't eat as much when they get nervous, and near as I can tell, those damn trespassers are making 'em nervous. Better, now. Hope they keep away."

Elaine nodded. "You call if they don't."

"You betcha."

Back in the car, once again on the gravel county road, Devlin asked, "Do you think they'll stay away?"

"For now. They must feel like we're crawling all over them. First the trespass warning, then me questioning them at Maude's and now dropping by when they're camping?"

He chuckled. "*Definitely* all over them."

"The question is, how badly do they want to watch those damn lights?"

"Any idea what they might be?"

Elaine shook her head. "I thought they must be a fire the first time I saw them. The thing is, though, I've lived here my entire life, and I never heard anything about those lights before. Never saw them."

"So they've never caused any concern?"

"Not until these UFO hunters showed up."

"I guess that would do it." The same way the arrival of strangers could cause problems when he was on assignment overseas. Hostiles? Innocents who just happened to be there? Definitely people to be watched.

But UFO hunters hardly seemed like the biggest threat. More like nuisances.

Elaine chose another turnout, one surrounded by spring trees and firs that created a palette of greens beneath the blue sky.

A small, weathered picnic table sat beside a black-ened firepit.

"This is kinda fancy for a simple turnout," he remarked.

"A lot of people have to travel long distances out here. These turnouts were probably used more often in the days when not everyone had a car, but they're still useful."

"It's a great idea." Welcoming, too. Boy, there was a lot he didn't know about the place where he'd grown up.

Maude had made their picnic easy to lay out: cardboard containers on the table, a couple of double-lined cardboard cups filled with lemonade, some plastic utensils.

"Maude's really moving into the environmentally friendly age," Elaine remarked. "Folks still want that foam, though."

"I remember when I was a kid and sometimes Mom would bring home dinner from Maude's. Man, did Caleb and I get excited at the sight of those foam containers."

Then he wondered if he'd made a mistake by mentioning Caleb. A shadow passed over Elaine's face, then vanished. "There's a whole lot I never learned about you guys growing up. Caleb wasn't one to talk, except about the present and maybe some about the future. Lu's told me more, but..." Elaine shrugged. "I guess your childhood doesn't matter that much."

An interesting thing to say, Devlin thought. "I don't think much about it," he admitted. "Not that it doesn't matter—only that most of it isn't relevant right now."

Elaine bit into her BLT and quickly dabbed at the tomato juice that ran down her chin. "I can see that," she said after she'd swallowed. "I'm not focused much on my childhood, either. It's just this feeling that I never got to know Caleb as well as I might have and then he was gone."

She looked away swiftly, hiding what he sensed was a sudden attack of grief. He let her have the space she needed and admired the woods once again as he ate his ham sandwich.

She was right about not knowing Caleb that well, he realized. Caleb had been his brother, yet over the past decades, they'd become virtual strangers, separated by their paths in life. Even as children, they'd pretty much had their own lives because of a five-year difference in their ages.

He felt his own sorrow, too, for a loss that couldn't be repaired. Brothers, yet not, separated by time and experience.

He looked at Elaine, who was continuing to eat her lunch. She'd gotten past her moment; now he had to get past his own.

"You need to ask Lu," he said.

Elaine looked up at him. "About what?"

"About Caleb. About the things you want to know about him. Nobody ever knew him better."

At that, Elaine smiled. "A mother is usually the best source."

"Up to a point," he agreed. "Right now I'm more interested in these UFO hunters of yours."

"Ah, don't blame *me* for them."

He laughed. "No such thought. No, I'm just curious about what makes people spend night after night watching the sky for something as weird as lights. I'd understand watching for artillery or some kind of air attack. Hell, I even understand plane spotters, those people who record tail numbers and can put together a plane's entire flight history. But watching a couple of lights?"

"I don't know." Elaine closed her container and pushed it to one side. "Maybe they expect something more to happen."

"Little green men?"

She grinned. "Or maybe something as simple as seeing more of them, or seeing them fly in ways that a regular plane couldn't? Some kind of proof that they're not from around here?"

"I'd go with the last one. It makes sense. Visitors from another world. Hey, that could actually be cool."

"It makes me think of those B movies from the fifties." She giggled. "Giant ants. Aliens in weird costumes. Queens who looked like they should have been in burlesque shows."

"Hey, I used to watch them when I was a kid. Mom liked to watch them with me. Man, did we laugh."

"Caleb didn't watch with you?"

Again he felt a pang. "Naw. He liked to read. Science fiction, for the most part."

"So not that far away from the movies you and your mom watched."

"Mentally, no. Except, as I learned over the years, the ideas in those books and in the magazines were far more intelligent than the movies."

"Where every problem could be caused or solved by a nuclear weapon."

"There was that."

They fell silent. A breeze began to rustle through the trees, lowering the temperature a bit but sounding almost happy. *Happy.* Something he hadn't felt in a long while. Elaine probably hadn't, either.

"What about *your* childhood?" he asked. A sister-in-law about whom he knew nothing. She must feel the same about him.

"Happy enough," she answered. "Friends, family. I had no idea that anything was wrong until my parents split and headed in opposite directions. Cassie can't travel, so they have to come visit us, but…" She shrugged. "New lives, new families for them."

Now *that* sounded sad—more like abandonment than anything else. "How old were you?"

"Fifteen. One of my teachers took me in." She smiled. "A long time ago, no permanent scars."

Maybe not. But nonetheless, he sensed something underlying that cheerful rendition. Of course, seeing past facades was an essential part of his job. Necessary to his survival and the survival of the people he worked with. Except for one serious misjudgment, for which he might never forgive himself.

"Which teacher?" he asked. "I'm testing my memory."

"Edith Jasper. The one with the Great Dane."

He nodded and smiled. "The dragon English teacher."

"That's her, all right."

"And Bailey? I always loved that dog."

Elaine shook her head. "Moved on, I'm afraid."

"Man, that must have been hard on Edith."

"I'm sure it was. She has a new dog, though. Harlowe. He's as big and gentle with her as Bailey was. It's a kick to see a woman that age walking a dog almost as tall as she is. But Edith likes to say that the dogs understand her limitations, and they sure seem to."

"Dogs are smart," he allowed. He'd seen strays using every wile they possessed to survive on the streets in places where they were despised.

Their lunch was coming to an end. Devlin took another look around—situational awareness, ingrained in him for years. Nothing here. But he still felt the faintest sense of threat.

Ridiculous, he told himself. A habit that just wouldn't quit.

But he still couldn't quite dismiss it.

As he wrapped up their leftovers and shoved them into the paper bag, he asked, "Mind if I come to the meeting with the UFO guys at Maude's on Tuesday?"

"No, it's not going to be official business. But why are you interested?"

He couldn't say that he wanted to get a feel for these people. A chance to see what might lie behind the apparently innocent UFO hunters. Because trust didn't come easily to him. No way.

"Just curious," he answered. "I probably won't ever see another UFO hunter again."

"I hope not," she said dryly. "I'm still waiting for the grapevine to pick this up. In a few days, we'll have little green men, werewolves and any other spooky things people can talk about."

He grinned. "What would all those have to do with UFOs?"

"Why would anyone think those red lights are UFOs? You want them to be UFOs, they need to do something."

"But what *are* they?" he asked as they strolled back to her vehicle.

"That's the question, isn't it? That's why they're here. I, for one, doubt the mystery will ever be solved."

But Devlin wasn't one to ignore a mystery. Mysteries were a big part of his life. They were just about more important things than some lights in the sky. Regardless, he'd always had trouble ignoring any mystery.

There probably wasn't a solution to this one, but he wouldn't give up until he'd checked out every avenue. At least it would give him something to do while he was riding out his enforced invisibility during his stay here.

"What exactly does Sally do for Cassie?" he asked as they drove back toward town.

Elaine compressed her lips.

"I'm sorry," he said immediately. "None of my business."

"Why not? You're her uncle."

He blew out a long breath. "I've been a lousy uncle."

"Trust me, I understand that your job keeps you away. Caleb's did, too, only he was closer and could come home for a few days at a time. You're oceans away. Nor are we very high on your radar. I'm sure you have a life of your own. Wife? Kids? People who need your attention."

Hardly, he thought. There was the job. Pretty much *all* there was, under the circumstances. "No wife. Not anymore," he said. "No kids." The only wife had taken a hike after one trip overseas with him. Not her taste at all, not even inside embassy walls.

He'd never wanted to attempt that one again. A woman could either travel with him—but only to safer places—or wait at home indefinitely. Not fair, no matter how he looked at it, and he certainly looked at it differently since his marriage blew up.

Other people managed to meld the job with a relationship, but most of them had married within the department. After his divorce, though, he'd never felt the urge to try again.

"Sally?" he repeated.

"She's a trained therapist for autistic children." Abruptly, Elaine pounded her hand on the steering wheel, astonishing Devlin. "I don't like those labels at all. What good do they do? Cassie's just Cassie. The way she is. Labels shouldn't define her, not to anyone."

He'd never thought about that, but he had an inkling of her frustration.

"It's pigeonholing," she said continued angrily. "Like it solves anything. Now they call it a 'spectrum.' *Where on the spectrum is your child?* What the hell does that help?"

"Maybe understanding from others?" he suggested cautiously.

"They don't understand regardless. It's just a label they can put on a kid, then not deal with it. Those of us who *are* dealing with it are dealing with individual children. Children who *are* individuals."

He waited, letting a mile or two pass by before he spoke again. "I take it Sally understands that?"

"Believe it. She tailors everything she does specifically to Cassie. Damn, I wouldn't let her near my daughter if I didn't believe that."

He absorbed her anger, understanding it the best he could. Since he couldn't really imagine how Cassie's condition affected her mother, his understanding was limited, other than sometimes seeing Elaine's pain.

But labels? He was aware of them, the dangers of relying on them. In his world, labels could cost lives. But was it the same with a medical condition? Labels might help there.

A spectrum, he thought. He'd heard that more than once, never much thought about it. But didn't the whole idea of a spectrum include Elaine's insistence that Cassie was an individual and needed to be treated as such? Maybe that was why the term had been created?

But it was still a kind of label, he supposed.

Then he stepped where only a brave man—or a fool— would go. "Will Cassie's condition change as she gets older?"

He anticipated an explosion, a justifiable one, but he needed an answer to assess the situation, and assessment was a part of his job that had been tattooed into his brain.

"I don't know," Elaine answered between her teeth. "No one can know. But that's what Sally is trying to help with."

Subject closed. He could hear it in her voice. Despite

being Cassie's uncle, he'd sacrificed his position in the family. He was entitled to nothing from Elaine, not even information about his goddaughter.

For the first time he could remember, he looked back over his life choices and wondered if he'd been a fool.

Devotion to country was one thing. Devotion to family was another, but maybe every bit as important. Maybe more important.

Chapter Five

The UFO hunters had proliferated almost as if by magic on the streets of Conard City. Elaine hooked her thumb into her gunbelt and just shook her head as she watched them. "This could get interesting," she said to her fellow officers.

Why wouldn't it? There were not only the groups who appeared to be "serious" about their hunt but also those who had come looking for some kind of party. Green alien heads dotted the landscape, along with other strange costumes. Their music was getting loud, too.

If she'd thought that first group was a small invasion, this crowd looked like the real thing. Not enough motel rooms, of course—not that that would have made much of a difference. Every road near the Bixby spread was filling with cars and tents. The hours were filled with excited voices. *Bixby must be ready to have a cow of his own,* Elaine thought, remembering that shotgun of his.

Gage had doubled the patrols outside town and increased coverage in Conard City itself. The force was stretched to breaking.

Then she headed out for her patrol along the ranch land, stopping by the house to ask Devlin if he wanted to ride along.

He did.

THE TWO WOMEN noticed the increasing numbers of UFO hunters in the city, and as the group had grown, it had become wilder and more fanciful. For Kalina and Zoe, the task of blending in had gotten easier. They eased their way into the fringes. No one even questioned their accents. In fact, the mob seemed delighted that others had come to view the lights.

"The more, the merrier," a guy wearing a mask with bug-like eyes had declared. He'd tried to give them cans of beer but they'd managed to slip away without offending him.

Which was fine with Zoe and Kalina. They were on a mission that had nothing to do with stupid lights in the sky.

According to Lance—the man who had seemed to have made himself the leader—more people were on the way. Nearly fifty, he judged, bragging to Zoe. She smiled and nodded appreciatively, aware that more people would make it easier to hide within the crowd.

For now, they had moved to a small campground near the base of a mountain, little more than a turnout from a gravel road, and were going out at night with others to try to see those lights and photograph them. Kalina and Zoe couldn't care less about all the fancy cameras or the lights, but they had to act excited themselves. Lance gave them meters to use since they had no useful equipment of their own except for a cheap camera. Meaningless meters, as far as Zoe and Kalina were concerned, but they pretended to be thrilled with them.

Who cared about infrared? So the lights were hot? Or they might have magnetic fields? The UFO hunters weren't getting any useful information out of those things, as far as the women could tell. The lights appeared to move just a little, sometimes fast and sometimes slow. Then they disappeared, winking out. And that was it.

Zoe and Kalina weren't amazed. They knew how things could appear to move because eyes jumped a little all the time. As for being impressed, they simply weren't. At all. Even when their new companions started whooping with glee because that infrared camera had caught a shape in the hot ball of light.

The lights posed no threat, so the women didn't care about them. They'd seen a lot of terrifying things in the sky at home, and these were a joke. Unfortunately, they felt they were wasting time on this game. Yet play it they must, because it afforded them a chance to go into town, to casually ask people about strangers.

This UFO thing was a stupid rich-man's game. They knew about life-and-death situations and were sure these people couldn't even imagine living that way.

But they remained stuck. They didn't know what the man they sought looked like. They'd expected to hear about strangers in such a small town, but the only strangers they'd found were the members of this group. And none of them could possibly be their target. It might have given the women ease of movement, but so far they'd learned nothing useful, unless one wanted an encyclopedia about orbs.

So they sat with the fools at night, a distance away from them, acting shy and modest, and whispered to each other. They were beginning to wonder if they'd been pointed to the wrong town.

All of a sudden, the task they'd set themselves seemed a whole lot bigger than when they'd left home.

But then, this country was overwhelmingly big. How

did you ever find a single person? It would have been hard enough in their own, smaller country.

Had they been directed here for some other purpose than the one they intended? But no, their informant could not have counted on this group of strange people seeming to come out of nowhere. Besides, she had helped them get the gun they carried. They trusted her because of that, mostly.

Glumly they watched those boring lights and tried to figure their way through all this. They'd had support at home, but they had no support here.

Two women, all alone. For the first time, they really felt it.

Then they scraped together some of the money they'd brought with them for a cheap used camera. That sealed their position in the group. It also made it possible for them to take pictures in town. That *could* be useful.

But they still couldn't believe how easy it was to get into this absurd group. Their first appearance had been received pleasantly enough, if a bit doubtfully. They could understand that, given the craziness these people were chasing.

But now, buying some camera equipment had gained them full membership. They no longer stuck out at all. Both thought their welcome had been too easy. They came from a world where trust had to be earned, not just given.

There was a disadvantage, however. It wasn't long before they realized the locals had begun to stare at the group as if they'd come from a different planet.

Which, in a way, Zoe and Kalina had. But apparently, united interests had allowed them to join the growing crowd of newcomers. And the bigger the crowd, the better the concealment.

Except it made it harder for them to pick out their target.

WHEN ELAINE ARRIVED back at the house, Sally had already departed, leaving behind a note with suggestions for Cassie. Lu had left another note saying she had taken Cassie for a walk.

The house was quiet, too quiet. Except for the virtual stranger who had walked into her life only a few days ago. He was a good-enough guest but still a guest. Still made her slightly uncomfortable, the way having company always did. Like you constantly had to be on your best behavior or something.

But when it came right down to it, Elaine decided he must be feeling much the same way. Not a single item of his had migrated from the office he was using as a bedroom. The one time she'd glanced in, she noticed all his clothes were still packed in his duffel, despite the closet with hangers in there.

She had no idea how long he'd be staying. Nor, she guessed, did he. He'd said something about being here for a while but still hadn't unpacked.

One thing was for sure—if he was going to hang around a few weeks, it'd be much more comfortable if they could get past the hostess-and-visitor stage.

"Thanks for dragging me around the county," Devlin said.

Amused in spite of herself, she answered, "Just one tiny little piece of it."

"True, but it reminded me of when I was a kid here. That was what I wanted."

"I'm going out on the porch. Join me?"

Together they went out front to sit on the wooden rocking chairs. One was small enough for Cassie.

Elaine spoke. "One of the things I love about these older houses is the way they have front porches. Newer houses focus on the backyard. Usually fenced. But these front porches—they're great if you want to see your neighbors, maybe chat a little."

"And pick up on the gossip," Devlin said wryly.

Elaine laughed. "Well, that, too."

"Any gossip about the UFO hunters?"

She shook her head. "It hasn't started to roll. Maybe so far, they're being viewed as transients."

"Or Bixby hasn't phoned everyone he knows about the kind of nuisances they are."

"That could be, too. But if all people see of them is when they show up at Maude's to eat, there's not going to be much to gab about, is there?"

His answer was dry. "Never knew that to stop a grapevine."

He had a point. "But the grapevine here isn't usually malicious or full of lies. Don't ask me why. You'd think the creation of something salacious would get everyone's interest. Ah, give it time. Those guys will start headlining out of sheer boredom, if nothing else."

"Some real information would be useful."

She looked at him, wondering at this trend in his thinking. "What 'real information'? They're a group of slightly wacky people. They probably believe in some conspiracy or other, most of which are basically harmless."

"Conspiracy theories aren't always harmless," he remarked. "Take a look sometime. Most are pretty much anti-government whether they have a good reason or not. Whether they seem threatening or not."

Elaine turned that around in her mind, considering the conspiracy theories she'd heard. "I guess you're right. No matter what they're about, they seem to claim the government is hiding something. Failing to do something. At least, the ones I know of."

He twisted in his seat, looking at her. "I'd be the last person to say that all governments are good, that they never do anything wrong. Of course they do. They're run by human beings. But to just theorize wrongdoing in the absence of real evidence, that could be dangerous. Anyway, in the course of things, I doubt alien conspiracies are a big problem."

Elaine nodded. "Well, other than some trespassing, I don't see this group causing any major trouble. They actually seem kind of harmless to me."

Then she saw Lu and Cassie walking down the street toward her, Cassie holding Lu's hand, one of those rare touches Cassie permitted. Her heart leaped as it always did when she saw her daughter. Cassie bounced a bit as she walked, but skipping was, as yet, beyond her. Lu waved cheerfully.

Did Cassie's step quicken? Oh, Elaine hoped so. Among her greatest joys in life were the moments that Cassie evinced even the smallest amount of happiness at seeing her. Or like the moment she had first said, "Mommy."

God, she wished she could lift her daughter into her arms and make all the bad things go away. She hated the feeling that her little girl was locked away somewhere inside a brain that couldn't share itself. A prisoner.

No, she couldn't afford to think like that. No way. Allowing sorrow to shadow her every day would do no one any good.

When Cassie and Lu reached the bottom of the porch steps, the girl's face brightened a little, and she said, "Mommy."

Oh, God. Elaine's heart squeezed with painful joy. "Hi, Cassie. Enjoy your walk with Grandma?"

Cassie didn't answer. Instead, she concentrated on climbing the steps.

"We had a lot of fun," Lu answered. "Squirrels are starting to run around with some spring fervor. An occasional brave soul of a bird singing its little heart out. Cassie loved the squirrels especially."

Cassie reached the top step and walked over to her mother—space between them as always, but only a couple of feet. Better than even six months ago.

"And a dog," Lu said, shaking her head slightly. "Read that list Sally left. I think she might have lost her mind."

Dog? In her heart of hearts, Elaine knew what was coming. Sally thought a puppy might draw out Cassie's responses. Well, if it would, then that was what was going to happen.

"I think I should talk to Sally first," Elaine said. "To make sure I do the right thing."

"Couldn't agree more. Training can be a lot of work."

Elaine thought of all that Lu already was doing for Cassie and her, and hated the idea of adding a dog to those burdens. "Unless I can get one already trained." As she spoke, she instantly remembered Cadell Marcus, who raised dogs for police K-9 work and trained service dogs as well.

With advice from Sally about what a dog would need to provide, Cadell would probably be able to come up with something appropriate for her daughter. A dog that already understood basic house rules. "I'll talk to Cadell," she said to Lu. "After I find out what Sally wants."

"Cadell would be a good idea," Lu agreed. "I'm capable of a whole lot, but running after a puppy might be beyond me now."

"It's practically beyond anyone," Devlin remarked.

Lu walked over to him for a hug. "I should have let you have that puppy you and Caleb wanted so badly."

"And you had a lot of good reasons for saying no. At the time it seemed unfair, but looking back I can see you were right." He smiled. "In terms of care and training, it would have become *your* puppy. Caleb and I were already a handful."

Lu laughed. "You sure were. Besides, I couldn't afford the expense."

Elaine hadn't thought about that. Just how expensive could a dog be? Food, yeah. Vet…but how often? Toys? Medicines? Shots?

Ohhhhh man. She needed to do some research on this subject.

A glance at Devlin told her he'd had the same thought. He just shook his head his head slightly, more a gesture of sympathy than anything else.

While Cassie enjoyed cookies and milk—leaving a lot of milk on the table as she dipped the cookies, then carried them to her mouth—Elaine reached for the note Sally had left on the refrigerator.

It was cheery as always, punctuated by Sally's balloon-style exclamation points. Sally loved exclamation points. But then, she lived her life that way, with a whole bunch of zest Elaine sometimes envied.

Today's note was full of positive descriptions of the minor ways in which Cassie had improved. Minor ways. Maybe sometimes undetectable when not looking very closely, not *watching* closely. Maybe infrequently enough that only an intensive therapy session could reveal them.

But that didn't matter to Elaine. Every small bit of improvement was like a warm ray of sunshine to her heart.

But then she came to the part about the dog in the note. Only it wasn't just the *idea* of a dog.

A dog might be good for Cassie, Sally had written. *The warm love always there is a good thing for anyone. It might slowly draw her out. On the other hand...*

Elaine almost stopped reading. That phrase rarely brought good news.

On the other hand, Sally's writing continued, *I think a cat might be better. A kitten, not too young. Cats have a way of remaining independent and often a bit aloof, which might be better for Cassie right now. Not overwhelming. Talk to Mike Windwalker about the personality differences. We can discuss it more later.*

Elaine looked up from the note. "You missed part of this, Lu."

Lu frowned faintly. "What?"

"Sally is also suggesting a cat because it might be more aloof. Which I guess I could see being better for Cassie right now."

"A cat, huh?" Lu didn't look very pleased.

"What's wrong with a cat?" Elaine asked.

"The way that they stare."

Elaine had to smile. "Like they know all the secrets of the universe? That's why the Egyptians thought they were gods."

Lu humphed. "Doesn't strike me that way." Then she sighed. "Whatever Cassie needs. I'll deal."

DEVLIN SAW ELAINE'S face droop at his mother's statement. She must worry that she was always imposing on Lu, but Devlin remembered his mother well enough to believe she'd moved in with Cassie because she was simply incapable of doing anything else. Lu had always wanted to be helpful. Of course, being helpful also gave her some control.

Stepping outside into the cooling afternoon, leaving the three inside to sort out whatever needed sorting, he realized his past had begun to haunt him. Mostly he kept it locked away, except for the lessons that had proved invaluable—ones he could never afford to unlearn.

But the emotional side of it? That was the part he needed to bury because no matter the purpose, he'd put peoples' lives at risk. His informants had a variety of reasons for working with him, and they all believed they'd never get caught, but sometimes they did. A personal nightmare he had to live with. A nightmare others had to live with, others such as their families and friends.

This last loss had cut him hard. Niko Stanovicz had been his informant for several years. A charming, fun-loving young man who concealed a strong devotion to one side of the war raging in his country. He might superficially act like it didn't matter, but it did. With every breath he drew, he wanted to make his family safe. At any cost.

Then someone had informed on Niko. This had resulted in not only Niko's torture and death but also the deaths of some of his closest friends. A stone running downhill, not caring what it killed in its path, and Devlin hadn't been able to do a damn thing to stop it.

Instead, he'd been yanked out before a mere conversation with him might put a target on anyone else. Because if Niko had been revealed, then likely so had Devlin. His entire informant network had to be rolled up and exfiltrated along with their families, forced to leave everything behind—but still alive.

He didn't like to think about all the lives ruined by one slipup.

One single slipup. But by whom? His bosses were looking into that, of course, but they might never figure it out. It might be as simple as one of Niko's friends having noticed something he considered suspicious.

There were places in this world where suspicion was a condition of life. Some of that had crept into Devlin as well. How could it not? In his life, trust wasn't easy to come by—it had to be earned.

The afternoon was waning into evening, but he felt no urge to return inside, even though the delicious aromas of dinner had begun to emanate through an open window.

He probably should go in and offer to help, but the size of that kitchen made it unlikely he could squeeze in or stay out of the way. Of course, he could sit at the table with Cassie. Maybe that wouldn't unnerve the child too much.

He wondered once again if it would have made much of a difference to have been here throughout Cassie's brief life. Then he thought of the distance the child kept between herself and her mother, and figured that even being here all along wouldn't have changed Cassie's problems.

Maybe he should do some research into Cassie's condition. Then again, that would probably only lead him into the thicket of labels that Elaine hated.

How would she react if he dropped one of those into the conversation? He couldn't begin to understand Cassie's challenges. All he could see was a terribly withdrawn child—but how withdrawn was she really? Was she more aware of all that went on around her than she let on? How did she fill up the inside of her head? Because he frankly couldn't imagine a brain ever going totally silent. So somewhere inside her were thoughts. Reactions. Feelings. Matters she couldn't share. How freaking lonely was that? Or was she possibly content being alone inside her own thoughts?

Crap. What did he know? How *could* he know anything? He suspected that Elaine was on a journey of discovery, too, watching the changes in her daughter, wondering what they might mean and if Cassie's situation might ever improve.

Tired of his thoughts and the pointless hamster wheel they were beginning to run around on, Devlin went back inside the house.

The kitchen smelled absolutely wonderful.

"Beef stew," Lu said over her shoulder as she stirred a huge pot.

"You always made the best."

"Still do," Lu laughed. "Cassie loves it, too."

Devlin pulled out a chair at the table and looked across at Cassie, who sat beside Elaine. For the first time, he noticed that Cassie's crayons were laid out in a neat row, all points upward. Similar colors next to each other. After each time the girl picked one up and used it on her new unicorn picture, she returned it carefully to the same place.

Devlin wondered how he might start a conversation without disturbing Cassie. What a curious thought to have. How could he have ever known that speaking might upset his niece?

"I guess Cassie loves unicorns," he remarked, then instantly wondered if Cassie might not like being talked about as if she weren't there. But how would anyone know?

"Right now." Elaine smiled. "Who knows what it will be next week."

"How can you find out?"

Lu turned from the stove, wiping her hands on a towel. "She'll just stop. Then we hunt through coloring books for something she *does* like."

Devlin nodded, then noticed something he hadn't really paid attention to before: Cassie was occasionally darting quick glances his way. He decided to address her directly. With no way to know if she was noticing, it seemed best to acknowledge her. It sure couldn't hurt anything. "That's a very complex figure you're filling in, Cassie."

"Adult coloring pages," Elaine said. "Fine detail. Cassie loves it. Don't you, sweetie?"

Cassie didn't answer. Her expression didn't even change.

"I'm thinking about getting her a set of coloring pencils. Better for detail. On the other hand, she might…reject them."

"Never know until you try," said Lu. "We got a ton of those coloring books on a shelf in her room. All we have to do is pull them out and see what she likes. Maybe the same for pencils."

How would they know what Cassie liked? Devlin wondered. Her face and expressions gave nothing away. But maybe all it took was Cassie starting to color one of the pictures. Right now she was all about unicorns. Next, maybe owls? Who knew.

In point of fact, though, he found he was genuinely enjoying watching her intense focus as she colored, the careful choices she made with the crayons. He was starting to develop a bit of intensity himself when it came to her drawing.

Cassie clearly didn't want to stop coloring to eat dinner. For a minute or so, it appeared she might have a meltdown, but it never came. Instead, she finally let Elaine move her picture and crayons to the sideboard, within her line of sight, and turned her focus to the bowl of stew placed in front of her.

She ate with the same intensity she had displayed when coloring.

Hyperfocus. That could be useful if it didn't dominate. He had a bit of it himself. Or maybe more than a bit of it.

Cassie fed herself, appearing indifferent but quite able to manage the small bites his mother had cut up for her.

"She's got some pretty good motor skills," Lu remarked. "Haven't you, Cassie? You worked hard at it."

"Yes, she did," Elaine said, a note of pride creeping into her voice. Then she looked at Devlin. "It wasn't easy."

Not easy for either his niece or his sister-in-law. A struggle for them both. He could almost imagine it. "How do you know what Cassie wants to do?"

Elaine shrugged. "She just won't do what she doesn't want to do. And pressing the issue tips her into anger. Into a meltdown. We try to avoid that."

"I imagine so." Because how could you comfort a child who wouldn't even accept a hug?

"So, a cat," Elaine said, returning to their earlier conversation. "I bet Mike Windwalker would have one with a calm temperament."

Devlin spoke, "It was interesting what you read from Sally's note. A cat would be more aloof?"

Elaine nodded. "That caught my attention, too. But a dog...well, dogs hate to be ignored. What if a puppy pushes Cassie too hard? Demands too much? I can see why Sally might be hesitant. I am, too."

She shook her head as Lu cleared Cassie's dish, then put the coloring supplies in front of the girl. Cassie dove right back into her picture.

Elaine left the table to help with the dishes. When Devlin expressed his desire to help, she waved him back to his seat.

"We got it," she said, smiling.

So he leaned back in his chair, wondering what the hell he was doing here. He hated not being busy, and right now he was anything but.

He also hated that his bosses had decided he needed to hide out in the hinterlands. Not that he wasn't glad to see his mother, and not that he wasn't grateful for this chance to renew his relationship with Elaine and finally spend time with his niece. Of course he was.

But that just wasn't keeping him focused and occupied to the extent he was used to. He closed his eyes, allowing the events of the past month to jam up behind his eyelids.

It had all happened so fast from the instant Niko had died. It hadn't taken long to learn that the young man had been exposed as an informant. And once they'd figured that out for certain, everything hit top speed. Getting Devlin out of there, checking to see if the info about Niko had traveled further. Then the roll-up of the entire network in that part of the world.

A great big hole in their global intelligence. A network that would take years to rebuild.

And the hunt for the informant. That was possibly the most important thing of all. Who had revealed Niko? And what if he or she had revealed others? They *had* to find the mole.

For his own part, Devlin thought his bosses were being hypercautious about *his* safety, though. He was probably at the least risk of anyone, because knocking off embassy attachés could bring a whole lot of unwanted attention, whereas Niko could have been killed for any number of reasons.

Hell.

AFTER DINNER, with the night growing chilly, Elaine joined Devlin on the front porch, in the rocking chairs that might have been there forever. They certainly had been there when she and Caleb had bought the house, dreaming of the evenings they could spend out here.

But she was troubled over Devlin. His continued presence, however good a roommate he was, bothered her. In all the years since she'd met Caleb, Devlin's visits had been few and short. Now he was talking about staying for a month?

As a cop, she'd long since lost any inhibitions when it came to asking personal questions. Well, except in situations where they might cause needless offense.

But being hesitant right now seemed ridiculous. "Devlin?"

He turned his head toward her. "Yeah?"

"Why did you come to visit?"

He didn't answer immediately. "To see Mom. And I thought it was time to get to know you and Cassie better."

She wasn't buying it. "How about right after Caleb died? Wouldn't that have been a better time? Your mom was all messed up. So were Cassie and I." Although it had been hard to tell exactly what Cassie felt, between her autism and her very young age. No, Elaine had just assumed the grief was there. She'd had to, in order to take care of her.

Devlin rubbed his chin. A neighbor and his dog were walking along the street, and Elaine waved, as did Devlin.

He was smooth, she realized. Very smooth. Easy with the social courtesies. Well, the State Department and all that.

He was also probably pretty good at lying. Wouldn't he have to be? How truthful could diplomats be, as a rule? They probably made a career out of skirting honesty.

But she was also pretty good at detecting lies, thanks to her law enforcement experience. She wasn't perfect at it—but then, most people weren't great at lying, either. Someone like Devlin would be, and she'd have to pay close attention. Very close.

Nor did it help that her attraction to him was steadily growing for some unknown reason. Good looking? Yeah. Attractive as hell? Oh, definitely. She hadn't reacted like this to any man since Caleb. But there had to be more than that, and right now she didn't fully trust Devlin. Simply showing up because he was Lu's son and Caleb's brother wasn't enough.

She sighed, thinking he was never going to *really* answer her question. That wouldn't help anything.

But then he spoke. Quietly, as if he didn't want to be heard by someone a few feet away. That quiet in his voice caused her skin to prickle with apprehension.

"I guess I owe you a little more," he said. "But I can't tell you much."

"Classified?" That wouldn't surprise her.

His turn to sigh. "Have you heard of classification of sources and methods?"

At that, her heart nearly stopped. She *had* heard of it, and she knew how closely guarded it was. Informants' lives depended on it. Intelligence gathering of any kind relied on the methods as well. A special place all its own in the layers of protection. "Then you can't tell me anything."

"I can tell you that somehow some of that information

leaked. But more than that? No. I probably shouldn't share even that much."

She looked at him, wishing the night illuminated more of him than just his eyes, but the shadows on the planes of his face, deeper in some places than others, revealed nothing.

"So you're here because…?"

"I needed to be out of the way until this gets sorted. That's all."

"Dear God," she said tautly. "Are you being hunted? Damn it!"

Without waiting for any response, she jumped up and stormed back into the house.

She didn't need a road map. If he was somehow involved in someone else's danger, then he might well be in danger, too.

And that could be dangerous for them all.

But as her fury eased, just a bit, another question struck her: Would his bosses have even let him come here if he was in any danger?

She heard his footsteps behind her.

"Elaine?"

"What?" She nearly snapped the word.

"I'm here so I don't inadvertently reveal someone else's identity. That's all."

"So you figure your own is already exposed?"

"Possibly. But right now no one knows."

She swung around, hardly caring at this point if Lu heard them. She'd probably be interested in all this, too.

"Then how is there no danger?"

He spread his hands. "In the first place, if anyone had thought I was personally at risk, I'd have been shipped to a safe house and cut off from everything. That didn't happen. I was told to take a vacation. That's it."

She nodded slowly, hearing but not believing. Not yet. The guy had to be a masterful liar.

He continued. "Additionally, given my position at the State Department, the bad guys don't want to screw with me. If they think they've got problems now, just let them take a shot at me. Not that anyone could track me here. Only my chief knows where I am."

She averted her gaze, thinking about it, trying to calm her racing heart and her fury. "So they just told you to get out of the way."

"Basically. For the safety of the people who work under me. I can't take the chance that I might slip in some way and reveal others. I have to stay way out of it."

It made sense, however twisted it might seem. And he'd probably just told her a hell of a lot more than he should have.

At last, her anger ebbed and common sense began to return. "Okay," she said. "But if you get one ping, one hint you might be in trouble, you get the hell out of here."

"I wouldn't dream of doing anything else." He lifted a hand as if he were going to touch her shoulder, then dropped it. Despite everything, despite her anger and the beginnings of a sense of betrayal, she was sorry his hand dropped away.

Then he said, "I'll leave in the morning."

The offer was tempting, until she thought of Lu. "You can't do that to your mother. Damn it, Devlin, she's seen so little of you. It's not right. You just practice your covert skills or whatever they are, and we'll get by just fine."

She started toward her bedroom, then paused to say one more thing. "And don't you dare stay away from Lu this long again."

Chapter Six

"Maybe being part of this crowd wasn't the best idea," Zoe murmured to Kalina in their native tongue.

"How else could we stay in this town without everyone staring at us and wondering?"

Zoe nodded, but she wasn't convinced—not anymore. As the group of outsiders had grown, so had the difficulty in picking out the stranger they needed to find. At first, it had seemed like there would be an easy way to blend in and look for this stranger, who didn't fit in with the small nutty group of people.

But now the crowd was truly large, with men of every age, so not even that would help, as they'd originally thought when the first people had appeared to be young. Almost as young as Niko, which made the women's hearts squeeze until it became hard to breathe.

And then there were all those people partying, wearing strange masks, which only confused the issue more.

Kalina spoke. "We may have a long wait."

"As long as it takes," Zoe said, her resolve in every word. "I'll wait forever to avenge Niko."

Kalina didn't disagree. If she did, she wouldn't be here.

But, Blessed Mother, she wished there were fewer people and fewer masks.

ELAINE CAME IN to the office early because downtown was becoming a problem for residents. Patrolling the roads had proved, so far, to be pretty tame.

Standing with her arms folded outside the station's door, she asked, "When are we going to limit the beer out there?"

"Can't do it," Stu reminded her. "Beer and wine are allowed in public, even with open containers. Just can't have 'em in the car."

Elaine shook her head. "This is madness, and it's getting worse. I don't think many people are enjoying this influx."

"It's not like Roswell," he agreed. "They make money off this kind of thing."

"These guys don't even think we have a crashed ship out here. What's with the lights? They aren't even interesting. They don't do anything."

Stu laughed. "Oh, listen to them now. Those lights are doing all kinds of things."

"I suppose. Somebody was talking about blue orbs yesterday."

"There you go. How long before we have little green men—"

"Gray," Elaine interjected dryly.

"Okay, the grays. And after that, we ought to be hearing about Bigfoot."

She turned to look at him. "What's *that* link?"

He shrugged. "I just heard that they come up together."

"That's all we need," Elaine said sourly. "And damn, I need to spend more time with my daughter. Makes me want to round up this whole crowd."

Stu raised an eyebrow. "And just where would we put them? You get on home and see Cassie. So far, these people don't look like they're going to create any real trouble. You can take a break."

"Except for annoying most of the local residents."

By this point, most of the in-town gathering had been occurring on the west end of the city, but a crowd kept congregating at Maude's diner, and she was getting truly frosted because they were getting in the way of her regular customers. Spending less, too. She'd probably be the next person to give Gage Dalton an earful.

Not many local residents wanted to breakfast with people who wore strange masks and costumes as if it were Halloween.

When she reached her own home, two blocks to the south of Front Street, where the big old mansions graced the road, the last of the revelers had disappeared. The usual quiet reigned.

To her surprise, however, as she pulled into her driveway, she saw both Devlin and Cassie sitting on the porch. *Cassie?*

It wasn't that her daughter didn't like sitting on the porch once in a while, but for her to be sitting with a relative stranger was quite something. A forward stride of some kind?

She approached slowly, not wanting to startle Cassie, who was totally absorbed in coloring. She sat in her yellow child-size rocker, with a small matching table in front of her. Just enough to hold her coloring sheet and her crayons.

Elaine's boots crunched on the gravel as she approached, and Cassie looked up with a small smile and said, "Mommy."

The word would forever cause Elaine's heart to squeeze. "Hi, sweetie," she said cheerfully. "I'm glad to see you decided to come outside." Then she looked at Devlin, who smiled at her.

"Cassie wanted to come out here and she's been happily coloring for the last hour."

"Did she follow you?" Elaine's heart skipped a beat with hope.

"You know, I couldn't tell you. Doesn't seem likely, though. I was out here for a while before Cassie showed up." His smile widened a shade. "So, how's the lunacy in town going?"

Elaine climbed the steps and sat in one of the other rockers. "It's going. A lot of these new folks seem to want a nonstop party, although I couldn't tell you why. The more serious UFO hunters—or researchers, I guess they're calling themselves—are parked up and down county roads, camping on the easement. The ones here in town..." She shrugged. "I can only say that the townspeople aren't thrilled by this."

He arched a brow. "Trouble?"

"Not yet. The revelers don't seem to be looking for any, at this point. Honestly, I'm not sure why they're here. It's not like we have some kind of history of this phenomenon. We're not on some kind of UFO map. No reason we should be. And all because of a couple of red lights that have apparently been here for years."

He tilted his head. "But no one knows what they are."

"Which means nothing." She shook her head. "Now, if we'd had a cattle mutilation or something like that, it'd be different. God save us from a cattle mutilation, though."

He rocked his chair slowly. It creaked a bit, but the sound was pleasant.

Looking down at the floorboards of the decking, Elaine saw another job that needed doing. The paint was peeling off. Maybe she should just scrape it all off and let the wood weather. She'd have to scrape it now anyway to apply a new coat.

Every time she turned around, she was aware of how little time she had to do things. How greatly some help would be appreciated.

Then she brushed the thought away. It would get done or it wouldn't. When she and Caleb had bought this house, they'd known it needed a lot of work. They had been excited about doing it, too. Except Cal was so often away, and Elaine's crazy hours didn't help much. Then Cassie...

She sighed quietly and looked at her daughter. She ought to be grateful, she supposed, that Cassie seemed so happy with her coloring. Or was she?

Questions like that would probably plague Elaine for years to come. Unless Cassie eventually learned to speak at least a bit about her feelings, they would always be a mystery.

Lu stepped out onto the porch. "I thought I heard you," she said to Elaine. "You're early!"

"Watching that crowd downtown didn't make me feel needed."

Lu sat on the last of the rockers and began rocking. "I'm glad they're not down this way. Nothing wrong with them, I suppose, but it feels strange to move through all those people, with their weird costumes. I'm just waiting for a bunch of new people to show up selling alien stuff, or whatever they call it."

"Now that would be a real headache," Elaine answered. Business licenses, shoplifting claims from kiosks that legally shouldn't even be there. No thanks.

"And what about drugs?" Lu demanded. "You know it can't be all beer and wine out there."

"Probably not." Elaine shook her head. "Unfortunately, unless we see something serious or smell something more than a little weed, we're going to have to let it go."

Lu made a sound of disgust.

"Look, Lu," she said, "us wading into that crowd because of a whiff of marijuana is going to cause a serious disturbance. How can we find the right perp to begin with? And if we start throwing our weight around trying to find out who has illegal drugs, we're going to have bigger trouble."

"I don't like it," Lu said.

"Nobody likes it, I'm sure," Devlin volunteered. "But why start a riot when it all still looks like a party."

That was a good way to put it, Elaine thought. Better than she had.

She looked at Cassie again and saw that the child had stopped coloring. Instead, she was looking at the adults. Nothing showed on her face, but she was clearly paying attention.

Another step forward? She hesitated, trying to figure out a way to encourage this change of focus without driving her daughter back into her shell.

After a minute, she stood. "I'm going to make some lemonade. Want to help me, Cassie?"

It was Cassie's turn to hesitate. She looked down at her picture and her crayons. Elaine held her breath.

"Cassie," Lu said, "if you want to go with your mommy, I can bring your crayons and picture inside for you."

A huge separation for Cassie. Allowing someone else to touch her beloved crayons and unicorn picture. Something she only allowed at bedtime. It wouldn't happen, Elaine thought. No way. Cassie would stay with her drawing and drink lemonade whenever it appeared in front of her.

But then, her heart climbed into her throat. Cassie stood, turned away from her drawing and walked toward Elaine. And ignored her crayons.

Elaine didn't touch her, fearing that might be too much, but Cassie followed right on her heels. A major break-through.

Everything else faded into the background—the UFO hunters, the weird party happening on the western side of town, the county road easements now full of people who wanted to see a couple of lights.

Cassie was taking a huge step. Nothing else mattered.

She looked at Lu and Devlin when they entered the kitchen. Cassie eagerly took her crayons back from Lu.

"Tomorrow," Elaine said, "if I can find the time, I want to take Cassie out to the veterinary clinic. Mike Wind-walker must have cats for adoption."

A positive step forward. Maybe. It would all depend on Cassie.

Then, her decision made, she went to call Mike.

DEVLIN HONESTLY DIDN'T know how he was going to stand any more of this bucolic life. Hanging around here for the last week had only reminded him of why he'd left in the first place. He needed to feel more active. To feel that he was accomplishing something.

Elaine had her job, an important one. His mom seemed happy buzzing around the house and taking care of Cassie and getting out into the garden, little by little, in the bur-geoning spring. Cassie seemed to like that, too, as much as one could tell what Cassie liked. She followed Lu out-side, without her crayons, and sat watching.

Damn, he wished he could do something for that child.

As for Elaine, she fascinated him. So strong. So powerful in her own right as a deputy. Seeming to need no one except help with Cassie. Probably explained how she'd endured Caleb's long absences when he was working a big construction job. Not as long as Devlin's absences, of course, but it was sometimes a month or more at a time with Caleb.

And Elaine had kept plugging along with her own life, her own activities.

But here he was, used to being involved and active damn near every hour of his days, sitting on a front porch, sometimes buying meals from Maude's and walking around a town that he knew but that would never be as familiar as during his youth.

Nope. Right now he fully understood the words *at loose ends*.

He hated it. Restlessness grew until he could barely hold still.

He wanted to call his chief but knew he shouldn't. You were hardly hiding if you started to call your contacts.

But the more he thought about this situation, the more he believed he'd been lied to. Sure, they wouldn't want him to have a high public profile, like that agent who'd been criminally outed all those years ago. That had put her entire network in danger and caused the agency to leap in and save everyone they could.

But there were also the innocent people, the ones who hadn't been her informants, people she had met in social situations. Had they been protected, too?

He had no idea.

That didn't keep him from feeling like he could have been more useful working on the problem of the leak than being here in the back of beyond, where he could do nothing at all.

The fact that that may have been the entire point didn't escape him, but he still loathed it.

Damn, he felt like a caged tiger.

Then a thought occurred to him. He could infiltrate those UFO nuts. A little research, a lot of practice from his career of blending in, and he could do it. He could find out what they were thinking and whether any of them posed a danger.

Not that he thought they did, but any one of them might. Some of them had to be truly unhinged. All it would take would be one.

He pulled his e-reader out of his duffel and went hunting for a few books, some more serious than others but quite a few on the edge of reality. They'd be the most enjoyable to read.

He loved to get into crackpot conspiracy theories. He'd even created a couple of them in his time.

Oh, they could be so useful in manipulation.

"WHAT ARE YOU READING?" Elaine asked later that night. "You've had your nose stuck in that reader for hours."

He looked up, half grinning. "I'm reading about UFOs."

"What?" She plopped down on the recliner and gaped at him. "You're not the type. Are you?"

He laughed. "No, not a bit. But…well, I thought I could understand some of what's going on out there."

She raised a brow. "Manipulate it, you mean."

He shook his head. "No. Wouldn't dream of it."

"Why not? Isn't that part of the reason you've been sent into hiding?"

He fell silent, compressing his lips. This woman was getting too close to a truth he didn't want to burden her with.

"What would you do with those silly people? Ramp

them up? Scare them? Make it all worse? Because you couldn't leave it alone, could you."

That last bit wasn't a question, and a coal of anger ignited in him. He set his reader aside on the end table. "I'm perfectly capable of leaving it alone. It's hardly my job."

"Then explain to me, Devlin. Just why do you want to read up on UFOs?"

"Are you aware that a few years ago, the federal government issued a report saying they were a number of cases for which they had no explanation? Cases with video and radar tracings?"

"I heard of it," she admitted. "They call them UAPs now, don't they?"

His reply was dry. "Only to dissociate the inevitable connection with aliens. There's absolutely no proof of anything like aliens."

"So you say."

His anger faded and he laughed. "And there it is. Whatever the government says must be one huge cover-up."

Elaine had to laugh, too. "I said that to get your goat."

"Didn't work. I'm used to that line."

She leaned back in the chair and curled her legs up beneath her. "So, why the reading?"

He leaned forward, placing his elbows on his knees. "Because almost invariably in any crowd, there's at least one person who's unhinged enough to cause serious trouble."

Elaine drew a breath. "A psychopath."

Devlin shrugged. "The word for it doesn't matter. The important thing is that some people get their thrills by causing trouble. Sometimes it's small problems, sometimes it's big ones."

"So what do you think you can do about it?"

"Join the party and listen."

Elaine stiffened. "You're going undercover with those guys? Are you kidding me?" Then she paused. "But that's what you do, isn't it?" She uncurled herself and stood up.

"I'm just going to listen," he said. And damn it, she *had* guessed more than he'd told her. She wasn't seeing him as some functionary on a purely diplomatic mission.

"You just be careful you don't draw the kind of attention that'll bring trouble back to Cassie."

Then she left the room. And Devlin once again considered moving to the motel. Except now it was overfull.

A sudden thought struck him: if any trouble came out of this invasion, he needed to be here to protect Cassie, his mother and Elaine.

That came first, before anything else.

He looked at his reader and wondered if he was being a plain fool to even think of infiltration.

ELAINE LOOKED IN on Cassie, as she did every night. The little girl was sound asleep, wrapped around a stuffed unicorn she'd had since infancy. The only stuffed animal she wanted. Elaine had no idea what she'd do when that cuddly doll could no longer be stitched together. Maybe a cat would help, but only tomorrow could solve that conundrum.

In the shower, she thought about Devlin. She'd detected the growing tension in him and felt that now she understood it. He wasn't good at sitting on his hands. Well, neither was she.

But to involve himself with that UFO crowd, especially the ones in town who took the alien ideas seriously? She supposed they should be expecting the media any day, the media with their cameras. And if this crowd hadn't

bothered the locals sufficiently, an invasion of TV people
would finish the job.

With a towel wrapped around her medium-length dark
brown hair, she sat on the bench at the foot of her bed and
began to apply skin cream. This was a dry climate, and
cream, especially on her hands, was necessary. She had
chosen the most odor-free she could find because she
suspected a deputy running around smelling like roses
or lavender wouldn't have the same authority.

She thought about Devlin again as she ran a brush
through her hair. She was thinking entirely too much
about him. Like she thought of Cassie. Not as much, of
course, but too often. Cassie was her life. Devlin was a
ship sailing through it, gone in a few weeks when he no
longer needed this safe harbor.

Well, she hoped he left, because she kept sensing danger around him. It was a feeling she had so far mostly ignored, as if it weren't there, except for that one time when
he'd said he would leave because she was angry with him.

Now this. In theory, this attempt of his shouldn't bring
any danger to the rest of them. That group of people
seemed pretty much harmless, if wacko. But as much as
they irritated some of the locals, others seemed to be enjoying the show as if it were a big colorful parade.

Elaine wondered how long that would last. Or how
long the crowd would stay out there. The fun had to wear
off at some point. And some of them must have jobs to
get back to.

Sliding into a nightgown and under her comforter, she
stared into the night, her ears always on alert for Cassie.

But her mind roamed far afield, to what it must be like
to work for the State Department, maybe to direct agents

who persuaded people to inform for you, to keep intelligence flowing your way.

What it must be like to lose one of them.

Closing her eyes now, she thought of what Devlin might be feeling. He'd never expressed anything about it, but he wasn't a cold fish, as far as she could tell. So it had to be affecting him. Had to concern him that a man he had worked with had been betrayed. Who had betrayed him?

No wonder his bosses wanted him so far out of the way. If someone was leaking information, they might leak his whereabouts if they discovered them.

God, what a mess.

In the morning, as she was trying to persuade Cassie to pull on her jacket for a car ride, Elaine had another thought about Devlin.

Yeah, she was worried that his actions might draw trouble to this house, but she suddenly turned the thought around: she was a deputy watching over those partying alien fanatics. *She* could just as easily draw their attention. Maybe more easily than Devlin. She could be targeted simply because of her uniform and her role.

Then she shook her head. No reason to think anyone might do such a thing in that group of people, who seemed primarily interested in having a good time.

They were just having fun, and the two lights provided the excuse.

But why hadn't they gone to Roswell, the place where these things usually happened? Maybe they just wanted something different, some place that didn't already have diners playing up to them, or a museum of questionable artifacts, or places selling all kinds of kitsch.

In short, a fresh, untainted place to stamp a new mark.

God, she hoped this didn't become some kind of regular thing.

"Mind if I ride along?" Devlin asked as he emerged from his room.

"Let's see how Cassie reacts once I get her into the car."

"Fair enough."

At this stage, Cassie wasn't keen on leaving the house. She might occasionally take a walk with Lu or her mother, but she wouldn't go into the park or into a store, and she pulled away when people got too close.

But then Elaine found an amazing key. "Cassie, we're going to visit Dr. Windwalker so you can get a kitty, if you find one you like. A kitty for Cassie?"

Interest flickered in her daughter's blue eyes, and she stopped resisting the jacket she knew would take her from her beloved coloring.

In what seemed like no time at all, she was fastened into her car seat, an amazing thing all by itself since Cassie usually hated to be restrained. But she knew the car seat from doctor's visits, and while she sometimes might kick up a fuss about it, she still allowed herself to be strapped in.

Nor did she object when Devlin climbed into the front passenger seat. Lu waved them off with a smile. She had plans to spend this free time with her friends.

"I feel awful about Lu," Elaine remarked.

"Why?"

"Because she's given up everything to look after Cassie. Sure, I can take over when I'm not at work, but it still limits her. She's always been outgoing."

"And she's always been capable of saying no. She's also perfectly capable of saying she wants you to hire help."

Elaine nodded slowly. Lu had certainly moved *herself*

in to help Elaine and Cassie. She hadn't been asked, not that her decision had upset Elaine in the least. But it *had* been Lu's decision.

Cassie made some random noises from the back seat. Rare vocalization, but always welcome. Then there was "Mommy." A relatively new word. *Not often enough,* Elaine's heart said, even though her brain knew she ought to be grateful it was happening at all. There would be other words. There *had* to be.

"So," she asked Devlin as they drove from town toward the east, which spared them contact with the revelers, "what have you learned from your UFO research?"

A smothered laugh escaped him. "Plenty, little of it flattering. I was focusing mainly on what's been happening in Roswell, New Mexico. Conard City is a long way from having to face that."

"Are you sure?" she asked.

"What do you mean?"

"Wasn't there just one reported crash out there? And they're still partying after all these decades."

"Well, some think there was more than one crash. But apart from that, there's a conviction that alien bodies were found. Or that they're alive and were taken to Wright-Patterson Air Force Base."

Elaine spoke dryly. "And of course, there's the government cover-up theory."

"At least they've got some reason for that. Are you familiar with the story?"

"Not much."

"So, consider that news of the craft crashing was on the local radio station, along with an interview with a rancher who found the debris. I think it was the same morning that the local newspaper reported that the public information officer at the air base had announced the crash of a flying saucer and said they'd found debris."

Elaine felt like she should have been aware of this. It sounded major.

"Then, a day later, the air force debunked the whole thing by saying it was a weather balloon and showed pieces of wreckage. And that's why Roswell has never been forgotten."

"Wow," Elaine murmured. "But we don't have anything like that here. Just a couple of lights."

"And no cover-up yet."

"I'm not sure I like the way you said *yet*."

But before he could reply, she turned into the gravel road that led to Mike Windwalker's veterinary clinic and hospital. She'd barely parked before Mike appeared, smiling. He wore green scrubs, and his black hair was tied back out of the way.

He came round to Elaine's side of the car and bent to look into the window. "I understand this is a bit delicate. What do I need to do?"

Good question, Elaine thought. She hadn't walked through this mentally yet, hadn't made a plan. "I don't know, Mike. I could use an idea." Especially since she feared a major change could lead to a major meltdown, over which she had no control.

He nodded.

"I've got one," Devlin said.

Elaine looked at him, surprised. So far, he had done not one thing to insert himself into Cassie's care. "What's that?"

"How about you and I get out of the car. Then Mike gives you a kitten to hold, and you take it to Cassie. What do you think?"

Elaine nodded slowly, then decided it sounded like the best way to go at this. "I probably should have just brought the kitten home with me. Getting it from here to there might cause a crisis. Damn!" Trying to figure all this out sometimes overwhelmed her.

"I've got a cardboard box with holes in it," Mike said. "Cassie and the kitten will be able to see each other. But first…"

He straightened and headed for the front door of the clinic. "I've got two," he said over his shoulder. "We'll try the second one if it seems necessary."

Elaine looked at Devlin, and they both climbed out of the car to wait. Cassie looked around her but remained silent. She was definitely interested in the change, though.

At last, Mike emerged from the clinic with a small bundle of fur in his arms, a gray tabby with bright green eyes. "Let's see how we do with this little girl."

Elaine opened the back door of the car and leaned in, waiting for Cassie's gaze to settle on her. "Cassie, we have a present for you if you want it. A little kitten. Do you want to see it?"

Cassie's gaze immediately brightened. Hopeful now, Elaine turned to take the kitten from Mike's hands and gently hold it out to Cassie. Instead of pulling away, her daughter reached out a hand to the kitten.

"Do you want to keep her, Cassie? Take her home with us?"

Cassie didn't answer, but reached out her other hand. Gently, Elaine rested the kitten on Cassie. The kitten dug in, clinging with her little paws and resting her head on Cassie. Purring.

And for the first time, Elaine saw her daughter smile—

truly smile. Her hand came to rest on the kitten, and her fingers moved gently.

Then Cassie said a new word: "Soft."

Tears prickled in Elaine's eyes, and she drew a shaky breath. "Oh, wow," she breathed. "Oh, wow."

GETTING THE KITTEN home took some effort. Cassie had to be persuaded to let go of her. For the first time, Devlin stepped in, as did Mike. Mike explained that Cassie needed to keep the kitty safe on the way home. That was what the box was for.

Devlin added that he'd make sure the kitty arrived safely, and if Cassie wanted, he'd sit in the back seat to watch the box with her.

Cassie allowed it.

Then Mike loaded up the back end of Elaine's vehicle with a litter pan, a small bag of litter, some cans of soft food and a couple of small toys.

Elaine didn't realize how tense she'd been until they were halfway home. She glanced in her rearview mirror, liking what she saw in the back seat. "Thanks, Devlin."

"I didn't do much. Truth be told, I'm still astonished that Cassie will let me this close. It must be the kitten between us."

"Maybe." But Elaine didn't think so. Apparently Devlin had been around enough to win at least some of Cassie's trust.

The only question was whether that would prove to be good. Or very bad. Elaine frowned. She knew she could become a mama bear if needed. She didn't want to have to do that with Devlin.

At home, Cassie settled on the living room carpet, just watching the kitten with fascination. Occasionally the little bundle crawled up on her and clung, accepting a light stroke from Cassie's surprisingly gentle hands, then resumed its exploration.

Lu returned from her coffee klatch and regarded this development with a small amount of suspicion. "I really don't like cats," she said. "But…" Then she smiled. "Cassie sure likes it. Has it got a name?"

"Not yet," Elaine answered.

"Then you'd better pick one. Or we can just keep calling it Kittie."

Which wouldn't be bad at all, Elaine thought. Cassie sure wasn't going to come up with one.

But watching her daughter play with the kitten made everything worthwhile. Cassie wasn't devoting the same level of intense focus she gave her coloring, but her focus was strong. More importantly, it was on something else.

Thank you, Sally, she thought. Better than a puppy, too. A puppy might have been too rambunctious.

No, the kitten was just right.

CASSIE FORGOT ALL about her coloring. Elaine didn't know if that was good or bad. It would certainly be good if Cassie could have two things to focus on, but exchanging one for the other? She wasn't at all sure about that and wondered if she should call Sally.

But then came another moment, a huge moment. The kitten grew sleepy and curled up in a ball. Cassie looked almost panicked, and Elaine was quick to settle down with her and explain that Kittie needed to sleep just like Cassie and Mommy did. Then, almost holding her breath, she asked if Cassie thought the kitten needed a blanket.

Cassie held up both hands, so Elaine hurried to get an

old, fuzzy afghan she'd had for years, maybe since child-hood. Didn't matter. The kitten would probably like it.

She spread it over the kitten, being careful not to cover its head. "See?" she said to Cassie. "All tucked in, but we don't want to cover her head." Although she doubted it would cause the kitten any problem. The blanket was porous.

"Okay? She'll wake up when she's ready."

Then she dared at last to go get herself a cup of coffee and return to her watch over Cassie. Devlin stood at the front window, and for the first time, she wondered why he'd been doing that since a while after they got home.

But she didn't dare ask when she looked again and saw that Cassie had pulled part of the worn blanket over herself and was sound asleep with Kittie.

Elaine's heart swelled as she smiled at her daughter sleeping with her new pet. Her daughter who had spoken a new word today: *soft*.

Then she realized what that said about her Cassie's development, no matter how hidden. And tears began to run down her cheeks.

DINNERTIME CAME, and Lu had to put up with a kitten roaming on top of the table.

"We can't keep that up," she told Elaine irritably. "But that's why I don't like cats. You can't train them."

"Sure you can," said Devlin. "I have a friend who has three cats, all very well trained about where they're allowed to go. It's okay. I'll get Kittie to stay off the table."

"But they like high places," Lu pointed out. "I know that much."

"Which is why I'll bring home a cat tree tomorrow.

Relax, Mom." Then he smiled. "Relax, *both* of you. Cassie will help me teach Kittie—won't you, Cassie?"

Cassie glanced at Devlin, amazing Elaine. Then she gave the smallest of nods.

Elaine looked at Lu, who had drawn a surprised breath. "Okay," Lu said, "that cat can dance on the table. For a while."

LATER, AFTER CASSIE'S BATH—with Kittie sitting on the edge of the tub—and after Cassie had gone to sleep with a cat curled up beside her, Elaine took her happiness to the living room, ready to share it, when she saw Devlin at the front window again. She could hear Lu in her bedroom, her TV turned on at low volume.

The night was once again filling with spring's seeping chill.

"What's wrong?" Elaine asked Devlin a bit querulously. "You've been staring out that window for hours."

He shrugged and turned to look at her. "Nothing," he answered.

"Sure, and I'm a werewolf."

At that, he smiled. "It's nothing, really. I saw a couple of those UFO types on this street earlier. They haven't come back."

Elaine turned her attention to the street, too. "Why are you waiting for them, then? You said they were basically harmless."

"I'm sure they are. But suspicion is practically engraved on my genes after all these years."

She had already gathered he was in some kind of secretive business, but the circumstances of everything he'd lived with hadn't occurred to her. No thought of what it might have meant for him. She edged toward the subject. "It must have been difficult, living overseas most of the time."

He didn't answer for a minute, maybe two. Then: "It had its good moments. Local people can be absolutely wonderful to nonresidents. Even Americans. In fact, I often think they have a better opinion of us than some of us do."

Elaine laughed quietly. "Why doesn't that surprise me?"

"The land of hopes and dreams," he remarked.

"And those weirdos you saw out there on the street? How are they being received?" Though she was wondering more about him than her neighbors.

"Probably my paranoia, like I said. Nobody else seemed bothered. Those two were likely just exploring for a change of pace. Although you'd think they'd take those masks off when they got too far from the crowd."

"You'd think." On that, she agreed with him. If they chose to look like something that might upset the locals, why leave the safety of the group? Why risk a bad reception from people?

But then, why not?

"We're a small town," she reminded him. "At least, small compared to other places—but a good place to get away in for a little while. You wouldn't have to go far."

"True. But I've been in smaller places. Much smaller."

She turned to face him again, deciding she'd tiptoed enough. Tiptoeing wasn't in her nature, certainly not as a cop. "Devlin? What the hell is going on? What has you on edge?"

Once again, he didn't answer, and this time his silence put *her* on edge. He was hiding something. He had to be. "Devlin?"

"Sorry," he said, wiping a hand over his face. "Like I said, bad habits. Learned responses. Nothing about right now."

She didn't believe him. She wondered if she should believe him at all, or if she'd ever be able to.

The thought made her feel ill. Devlin was her departed husband's brother. Lu's son. She shouldn't have to wonder about his honesty.

But now she did.

Turning, she went to knock on Lu's door. "I'm going to work for a while."

Lu answered groggily. "Okay, I've got the baby monitor on."

"Thanks."

In her own room, she put on her uniform and pulled her service pistol out of the gun safe.

As she passed through the living room, Devlin spoke. "I thought you had the night off."

"It's time to do some recon."

"I'll come with you."

She faced him once again. "I'm the cop, remember? I don't need your backup."

Walking out the door, she felt pretty good about herself. She'd just painted a necessary line and told him not to cross it.

Hell, she didn't need a man to protect her.

But the man came anyway, which irritated her. "I know you don't need me," he said. "You never have before, and there's no reason that should change. I'm just curious."

"Well, stay away from me," she said sharply. "You don't want to give the impression you're law enforcement."

"Nah, I'll take my own car."

As if he realized she could get into trouble if people

thought he was a deputy because he accompanied her. Maybe he did. Or maybe she'd pushed him away enough to make a point of his odd absence in his mother's life. His absence from Caleb's and Cassie's. It might have been his job, or it might have been self-absorption. How could she know? She just knew that her trust for him was shredding fast.

As he walked to his car, she said, "Watch yourself, Devlin. I don't want to have to rescue your butt."

Although she suspected he might be used to saving his own butt, probably by talking. Glib talking.

DEVLIN COULD FEEL Elaine pulling away from him. She'd never been in a hurry to get close, which he could understand, given his prodigal son routine over so many years. But now she was closing even that off.

He deserved it. He *didn't* deserve her trust. Trust needed to be earned, and God knew he'd done little about that.

He figured he was staying at her house only because of his mother, which was a sorry commentary on him. However, he needed to find a way to make at least some small amends.

As for the crowd downtown, he just wanted to see them. To take their temperature. On absolutely no mission he'd had overseas was a gathered crowd something to be ignored. Any group of people focused on a single thing was a fire waiting for a spark. Violence could break out at any time.

Even though these partiers seemed to be in good spirits and here just to have a good time, they were still a crowd.

He took his time driving to the center of town and

parked some distance away, taking care to approach at a casual walk.

He saw Elaine up ahead, talking to a small knot of people, making them laugh. She was good at this.

But he had a different perspective. She probably didn't see trouble, just a group who needed reminders to avoid any trouble.

Devlin saw trouble. In its nascent stages, to be sure, but still a huge potential for trouble.

And he didn't like the number of shopkeepers who stood outside their businesses with folded arms. None appeared to be carrying a weapon, but just because you couldn't see it didn't mean it wasn't there.

He turned to a couple of people in green outfits who were wearing the masks with big black eyes.

"Say," he said amiably, "is there somewhere I could get one of those masks? They're so cool!"

One of the aliens pulled back her mask. She was carrying a backpack, and she dropped it to the ground to paw through it. "I got some eyes in here. Best I can do, but nobody here is selling them. Not like Roswell."

He feigned something like excited interest. "You've been to *Roswell*? I've never been able to do that."

The young woman handed him a mask made mainly of cheap felt with two huge eyes. "You gotta find a way to get there. That party is a real trip. Every July, around the time the saucer crashed."

She gave him a wide smile. "It's not cheap. The place has really grown, hotels cost a lot—meals are cheap enough, though. If you go to the right places. If you come, find me. I'll show you around." Then she paused. "I guess I should tell you my name. Just look around for Alienne. Two *N*'s with an *E* at the end. Almost anybody knows me."

"That must be a lot of people."

She laughed. "The more, the merrier."

She and her silent companion were starting to move toward the center of the crowd, so he stopped her with a question. "What do you think about the crash?"

She shrugged. "Some of us believe it. Some of us think there are live aliens, some think there are bodies and pieces of a ship…" Then she laughed again. "Doesn't matter which story you want to believe. It's a great party."

Then she and her friend merged into the crowd. Devlin put on his mask and adjusted it so he could mostly see through the dark eyes, which were about like sunglasses.

Alienne, pronounced *alien*, amused him. A woman who believed very little about this whole issue but just enjoyed the partying. Not half-bad.

And about as fake as could be, given where she was. He would have expected some defense of one of the conspiracy theories. An impassioned one. Nope.

He turned a bit and picked her out of the crowd. Surprisingly easy, considering most of this motley crew were wearing similar costumes. She stood out anyway, being tall.

ELAINE BEGAN MOVING along the edges of the boisterous crowd so she could follow what was left of the sidewalk to talk to the shopkeepers.

Maude and Mavis were the first she met, and both of the large women looked as if murder wasn't far from their minds.

Maude spoke first. "There's gotta be a way to stop this, Elaine. Some way. I heard all that stuff about how it doesn't matter who shows up to eat, long as they all pay. 'Tain't true. I got regulars who can't get through my door.

Not as I blame 'em. But what's gonna happen if this keeps going on? Maybe they never come back."

Elaine honestly couldn't imagine that. Going to Maude's for a meal or just coffee was so ingrained in these parts that people were probably suffering from withdrawal.

Which meant what? That some people might try to take their town back? God, what a thought. Maude was right. They needed to find a way to stop this or at least shrink the numbers.

The UFO hunters out there along the roads seemed minimal by comparison. Although she wondered if Beggan Bixby would agree with that. So far, they hadn't gotten an annoyed call from Lew Selvage, though. If anything was happening on his ranch, it wasn't bothering him.

Or maybe he was burying the bodies.

The thought caught her by surprise, and she had to snort into her gloved hand. God, what a notion. On the other hand, Bixby...

"Damn," she nearly growled as she continued her stroll down the street, one eye on the crowd, the other on the annoyed shopkeepers. And more than one of them was able to justify his presence on the street.

But as the locals grew increasingly fatigued from protecting their property, trouble became more likely.

Chaz Rickard, who owned the organic-foods market, had a different take, though. He shrugged it off.

"Sure, I'll protect my windows, but they don't mean no harm, Elaine. Just an excuse for a party. Besides, I sometimes wonder about it myself, that spaceship crash near Roswell. Seems like the government changed its story in a whiplash."

There it was. The conspiracy. "I only heard a bit about that."

"Most people don't care. Why should they? Uncle Sam says it didn't happen, and that's all they need to make themselves happy."

"But you don't agree?"

Chaz shook his head. "Hard to, when they change the story. Now they released a report that said it was a weather balloon from some new program or other. Project Mogul, that's it. Anyway, records show they didn't launch any balloons for three days around that time. Hard to buy."

"It would be." She had to admit that much. Except where exactly was this info about there being no balloon launch coming from? A logbook of some kind? But those could be faked, too.

She suddenly wanted to laugh at herself. Now she was inventing her own conspiracy theory. Easy enough to do. Maybe some subjects just asked for them.

She turned around. Strangely shaped denizens of Zeta Reticuli, or some other planet, had disappeared. They were still clustering up near the center of town, which was no doubt making the sheriff's office unhappy. Maybe she should check in with her colleagues who were still working in town.

The remainder of the thinly spread force was trying to monitor the rest of the county.

Maude was right. In a lot of ways, this needed to stop. The city council was probably trying to write a new ordinance the sheriff could act on.

Yeah. First Amendment. Another laugh wanted to escape her. This entire situation was so ridiculous.

And so close to becoming a powder keg.

DEVLIN FOUND HER while she was still at the edge of the crowd. "Hey, Deputy. Recognize me?"

She looked into his green, bug-eyed face. "Gone over to the dark side?"

"Not exactly, but learning a lot."

"And?"

"They're mostly harmless. Mostly getting to the point of running out of money."

"Well, that's good news."

"Maybe. Some of 'em better consider transportation issues when they wanna leave. And of course, there are some hard-core types here. They honestly believe those lights are something from another planet."

Elaine bit her lip, then said, "So why aren't they out there with the other hunters?"

"I'm trying to find out. Probably nothing more important than that they really just want to have a party."

Which was entirely possible, he thought, scanning the crowd once again. The hard-core UFO types were camped all over the county watching a couple of lights. The rest here were mostly people who weren't hard-core but enjoyed the camaraderie.

Still, he remained uneasy, wondering what the hell was bugging him so much. There was nothing about this crowd that suggested they might be like the crowds he'd seen during his various assignments. Crowds full of anger, full of a desire for change no matter how bloody. Crowds just waiting for a match.

Which local governments gave them all too often. All it took was a bullet or two, or a bunch of soldiers marching in, to break it all up.

A lot of people lived on a hair trigger, often with some justification. But this group?

He shook his head. Maybe it was time to readjust his thinking. He was in a different world now.

"Is THAT HIM?" Kalina asked. Surrounded by loud, laughing voices, she had no need to keep quiet.

"I'm not sure," Zoe answered. "The informer said he was tall, but there are a lot of tall men around here."

It was true, Kalina thought, looking around. She and her sister were hardly bigger than children in this crowd. "How do they get so tall?" she wondered.

"Better food than we ate," Kalina said bitterly. "Better than Niko ever got."

Both women fell silent, recalling a past that goaded them, that angered them, that hurt them. Remembering parents who had tried so hard, only to be sacrificed on the altar of war.

Remembering Niko, who had somehow pulled the three of them to a better place, a place with a roof and regular food, however poor it might have been. Arranging for them to be protected when he was away.

A brother who had given them survival. Perhaps more than survival, because he had surrounded them with men who made sure nothing bad happened to them, surrounded them with women who had become mothers and sisters to them. People who had taught them how to take care of themselves.

Niko, who had never forgotten the importance of family. Niko, who had sacrificed himself, according to one of the men who looked after them. A man who got angry and shouted about Niko. A man they had feared until the day he looked at them and said, *Find the man who caused Niko to betray us. The devil who turned him into a* zradca. *The man who made us kill Niko.*

Two men? Or just one? When they had tried to find out, they'd been yelled at and told to find the American *diabol*. That it was their duty to their family. The only way to honor their brother. Their only way to pay their debt to those who had cared for them all these years. And the idea of vengeance was a good one.

The fear had followed the girls all the way across a war-torn country to an old man who drove them in a rackety truck to a border, where they boarded a fishing boat that carried them across an ocean. Then a much smaller boat sailed them along a misty coastline and dropped them on a ragged beach with only a map that had been rubbed almost to invisibility. By then, their fear had grown into fury.

They had no doubt that Niko had sold himself to save them. To keep them fed. To make life easier for the small community where they sheltered. But they could not escape the fact that whatever his purpose, he had stained their family.

Still, protected or not all these years, Zoe and Kalina had learned some things. They had learned to fight. They had learned to find their way along strange roads in unfamiliar lands. They had become warriors from necessity, because real protection didn't mean relying on others.

And for all these weeks, they had lived for a single purpose. To kill the man who had turned Niko into a traitor.

They'd had help getting close to him. It seemed the American *diabol* could be betrayed, too. And by one of his own.

A Slovak who for years had been working for the Americans, too, but in a regular job. A job where she got more information to pass the other way than Niko could ever have given the Americans.

The twisted story sometimes seemed impossible to the sisters, but they believed it anyway.

Now here they were, in a town that had suddenly turned stranger than they could believe.

And they had to become people who were very different from any they had known.

Americans had the security and the money to behave like this for fun? Or was it some kind of religious holiday they didn't understand?

MITCH CANTRELL, a highly successful rancher whose land abutted Bixby's, came to town a day later and entered the sheriff's office with a proposal.

"Just tell all those nuts outside town they can camp on my land. I got a parcel I'm not using this year just lying fallow, and it'll solve one problem. Folks are getting pretty annoyed out my way because the roads are being narrowed by all those campers. Can't get a good-sized truck and trailer through there, and we need to be moving cattle."

Gage Dalton liked the idea. "It would cut down on the number of people I need out there to keep an eye on things."

Mitch laughed. "Looks like you got enough trouble here in town. *You'll* need to move 'em, though. No way they'll listen to me."

ELAINE HAD BEGUN to grow seriously irritated. She ordinarily loved her job, and it usually offered her plenty of time to spend with Cassie, but these green, bug-eyed partiers were soaking up damn near all her time. Shifts were longer because they had a limited number of cops. Days off were canceled for the time being. Right then, the deputies were lucky to get a half day off.

Time with Cassie? Not enough of it.

Devlin joined her during the late afternoon as she was shoving some food in her mouth and changing her uniform shirt.

"I'd take the shift for you if I could."

She paused, her fingers on the buttons, and looked at him. Really looked at him for the first time in a couple of harried days. She didn't doubt him. Nor could she quite ignore the tingling attraction she felt for him. Caleb's brother? She was certain that would involve a guilt trip bigger than the state of Wyoming. "I'm sure you would."

Then, completely astonishing her, Devlin tugged her gently into a hug, his hands rubbing her back. "Elaine... No. Not now."

He stepped back. The loss of his embrace felt like her skin was being stripped away, more so because she knew exactly what he meant. Hunger, growing ferocious despite everything else going on. Damn, all she wanted was to fall into this man's arms and forget the whole world for an hour or two. Just shove everything away.

He was so good looking, so attractive, that she could barely withstand her own urge to pull him toward her, to demand he answer the needs that pounded through her body.

But he was right. Not now. She had a few minutes to spend with Cassie; then she had to get back to work.

"I hate this," she said suddenly, then turned away to go sit with Cassie and her kitten. Kittie was still commanding the kitchen table, curled up right beside Cassie while she colored.

Lu had given in, and there was no question that Cassie was looking happier.

Thank God for kittens.

Chapter Seven

When Elaine headed for the office the next morning, getting ready to organize the mass relocation of dozens of campers to isolated ranchland, Devlin insisted on riding along with her.

"You're going to need bodies," he said firmly. "All I have to do is stand behind you."

He has a point, she thought. He wasn't exactly the image of a guy who could be safely ignored.

"I won't interfere in any way," he added as they walked out to her patrol vehicle. "Your job. I'll be a fencepost."

Unless he decides something else is needed, she thought, but then she figured some ranchers were going to be out there, too. To *help* with the relocation.

She swore under her breath, considering all the trouble that could come from what had seemed like such a simple idea from Mitch Cantrell.

Yet the groups on the road hadn't seemed inclined to do much except try to sky watch. No parties, no drinking. A surprisingly sober group, unlike the crowd in town.

There was a lot of radio traffic as the deputies worked their way to the various groups. There were, as Elaine had worried, a lot of ranchers, too. Even those who weren't being hassled.

Radios continued to crackle as each deputy reached their appointed camp spot. A brilliant sky overhead made the day seem peaceful. Gentle, crisp spring air filled the whole area, dampened only by a few clouds of dust. Ranchers still arriving.

"This could get interesting," Devlin remarked.

"Maybe," Elaine answered. "On the other hand, the outsiders will be where they really want to be, and none of the ranchers should be bothered once they're on the Cantrell spread."

Devlin chuckled quietly. "That's the idea, anyway."

DEVLIN, FOR HIS PART, was pretty impressed by the calm with which Elaine approached this entire situation. Especially as they reached their appointed camp and five UFO hunters were facing three ranch-types. Hired hands? There couldn't be too many ranch owners out here. And if they were sending hired hands…

The back of Devlin's neck prickled. He had plenty of experience recognizing inflammatory situations.

Elaine climbed out, her gunbelt and baton in plain view despite her uniform jacket. In fact, she tucked her jacket behind the butt of her pistol. A subtle warning.

"Hey, folks," she said pleasantly, smiling. "What's up?"

Then she looked at the three guys in jeans, jackets and cowboy hats. "We're moving them. Isn't that what you want?"

Some mumbles greeted her.

"Exactly what I thought." She turned to the UFO people. "We're going to take you out to a place on the Cantrell ranch. It abuts the Bixby land you've been wanting to get onto. And you'll have a clear sky view, okay?"

One of the hired hands shifted. "No light out there for a fact."

The five UFO types exchanged looks. Elaine wished she could remember the names of the two of them she had talked to at Maude's, but they escaped her just then.

"Well," said the woman whom Elaine had believed was their leader, "that sounds good to me. We've got a lot of camping gear to pack up."

"We'll help," said one of the hands. "Them cars of yours ain't gonna get across the rough ground too well. You might need some help from our trucks."

Pickup trucks so old they looked like they might have been last painted fifty or so years ago. Plenty of dents, too.

But that didn't matter when the engines purred.

Devlin started helping fold up the camp and putting parts of tents, cookstoves and all the rest in the trunks of cars. To make it easier and quicker, some of the load went into the pickups.

What didn't leave the hands of the UFO hunters were their fancy cameras and other equipment. Devlin could understand that. A large chunk of someone's bank account had gone into the best money could buy, from cameras to special lenses to color filters. Then there were the magnetic field readers, and he thought he saw a Geiger counter.

The Geiger counter struck him as extreme, but he was prepared to shrug it off. After all, these people had come to the middle of nowhere because they'd heard of a couple of red lights.

Now *that* was extreme. Yeah, he was sure a lot of people wouldn't mind knowing what those lights were, but this kind of time and equipment devoted to trying to find an answer that would probably be mundane? If they even found one.

With the first group on their way down the road with the three cowboys, he and Elaine moved on to the next group. These people were feeling more threatened by the arrival of two cowboys.

Devlin could hardly blame them. These two cowboys looked a whole lot less friendly than the original three. Plus, this group of UFO hunters included four women.

He scanned them in the bright light of day, thinking he saw something vaguely familiar in one of the faces. He shook his head inwardly. At this point in his career, having seen so many thousands of faces, it might take only a single feature to cause a temporary misidentification. He always had to be wary of that.

Didn't stop the back of his neck from prickling once again, though.

This removal was a little more difficult than the first. These cowboys didn't feel like offering any help; they just made unflattering comments the whole time about the six people, mostly about the four women.

He could see Elaine gritting her teeth but not wanting to stir up trouble.

So he stepped in and started helping to break down the camp. As he did so, he remarked, "Just ignore them, ladies. Some guys just don't know any better."

He heard Elaine draw a breath. But the women relaxed a bit as they realized they weren't facing this alone. Then one of the boys with the UFO-hunters group said, "Yeah. I see it all the time at work. It's one way to get your jollies, I guess."

The guys getting their jollies looked pretty mad just

then, but a glance at Elaine in her uniform was enough to make them turn away.

"Tell the boss they's goin' away," one of them said as they climbed back into their rusty trucks. They jammed down hard on their accelerators, spraying gravel and dust everywhere.

"Well, that was pretty," Elaine remarked. "Thanks, Devlin." She offered thanks to the kid who'd spoken up, too.

The young man shrugged. "Easy to do when I had backup," he said, then laughed. "*Two* backups. I was just trying not to cause trouble."

A mature attitude, Devlin thought. *Very mature.*

"You know," that same young man said as they finished packing gear into trunks and car carriers, "we're moving. We got invited to a place to camp and keep looking at those lights. So why did those guys act like we were trouble? We're getting out of the way."

"Some people," Elaine remarked.

"Yeah, you'd know, wouldn't you?"

But Devlin noticed one thing. Two of the young women didn't look at all happy about going out to the ranch to camp, even though it would have to be better than camping by the roadside.

What troubled them? Feeling unprotected from all the guys who'd be out there, too? But there ought to be enough decent men to make sure nothing bad happened, and enough women to raise a ruckus if it did.

Bothered, he watched the crew depart, then looked at Elaine.

She'd sensed something, too. He could see it in the faint frown on her face. But then she tugged her hat to a more secure position on her head.

"Just one more group *we* have to move," she remarked. "The others must have moved their crowds by now."

"They've been springing up like weeds, huh?"

She grinned at him. "Maybe there's a shortage of spots for watching UFOs."

"Wouldn't surprise me, actually. But you're sure they know where they're going?"

"Yeah, they were already moving, which means Mitch Cantrell let 'em know where to go and probably has some hired help to guide across his ranch."

"Like a well-oiled machine."

She gave him another smile before they climbed into her Suburban. "Sometimes we get it right."

And sometimes people could get it very wrong. He slipped into the darkness inside himself, thinking of Niko, who'd only been trying to do what he believed best for his people. The kind of patriot one rarely met.

Too many of his assets had been interested only in money, a tidbit of info for some American dollars. Niko hadn't been like them. He'd brushed away the idea of money until Devlin had insisted he take at least some for the sake of his family.

Maybe the money had given him away, even though it had been in local currency. But a clue, perhaps, to the fact that Niko's family was living better than they had before.

God! What if his own insistence had brought Niko to the attention of the wrong people? It might well have, since the company still hadn't found a leak. Any leak.

Not that the CIA didn't have its share of them. Like in any huge organization, there were always people who saw a way for personal gain by sharing information, though usually not a lot of it and never revealing assets. Everyone, including the most venal, knew that assets were more than information sources. They were *lives*.

He felt gloomy anyway.

By the time they reached the entrance to the Cantrell ranch, a caravan was forming, ready to begin the trek to the land Mitch Cantrell had offered to let them use.

Cantrell stood on the bed of a pickup truck and whistled loudly to get everyone's attention. "Just a couple of things. I'm going to put a few of my men out there with you to keep an eye on some things. I don't want fires being accidentally started. Wildfires aren't a joke. You're going to clean up any litter. If you need bags, I'll provide them. And you cart your trash out with you? Got it?"

From the nods and murmurs, everyone got it, and most appeared to agree with the restrictions.

Mitch wasn't quite finished, though. "Livestock. Most of it is fenced elsewhere, but if cattle or sheep get through and come your way, just leave them alone. My guys will take care of it, and I don't want you scaring my animals."

Again, more nods. It appeared settled.

In fact, the groups were pulling together and talking in excited voices. A place to watch from. A place not polluted by light. A place where they didn't have to worry about being chased away by armed men.

Devlin looked at Elaine and saw her frown as she heard the group. "'Armed men'?" she repeated quietly. "Not here. Not yet."

"Well, there's Bixby."

At that, her frown vanished to be replaced by something approaching a grin. "He'd be the only one I'd worry about. Why do I get the feeling these people are talking about somewhere else?"

"Because they probably are. God knows how many UFO hunts some of them have been on."

They had begun their drive back to town, Elaine drumming her fingers on the steering wheel. "I never thought about those guys running all over to do this kind of watching. I also can't imagine what drives them."

Devlin gave it some thought as they turned onto a narrow paved road. The sun now came through the window on his side of the vehicle. Warm. Pleasant. A moment to be enjoyed, as so few were.

"I don't know," he said. "I probably should ask them. But I think they're hoping to see something that breaks all the rules. Something that hints at life beyond this planet."

Elaine sighed and shook her head. "Unless aliens want to land at the White House in front of all the TV cameras on the planet, I doubt we're ever going to have proof of that."

"Maybe not, but it's fuel for the imagination."

But there were limits to that, he knew. Limits to protect against very real dangers. Not on this alien-hunt thing. He didn't think those people were in any serious danger from UFOs or UAPs. The alien-abduction thing far exceeded his credulity.

The threat they faced more likely came from angry landowners than anything they might see in the sky.

But something was definitely wrong there. He'd felt it again, among those groups, though he couldn't localize it. Maybe someone in that crowd intended to do something that could bring trouble down on everyone's head.

Well, there was nothing he could do about it unless some information happened his way. And since he wasn't actively looking for it, wasn't actively trying to groom an asset, the chance that he'd hear something important was highly unlikely.

So he would relax and just enjoy the break from his duties.

Turning his head just a little, he filled his gaze with Elaine Paltier. His sister-in-law.

God, he ought to have guilt over his feelings. Ought to feel like he was betraying his brother.

But he didn't.

Sorry, Caleb, he thought. *She's alone now.*

More than alone. A single mom with a wonderful daughter who was going to need care for the rest of her life.

If Elaine thought about that, she must feel the weight of the future with Cassie. A weight that might become crushing, not because of needed care but because of emotional pain.

Because she loved Cassie and wanted a full life for her, and she might never see it. Or even most of one.

Devlin had missed Caleb many times over the years, and even more since his death because now there wasn't even a possibility of an email or a Skype conversation. All those avenues had been pruned.

But now he wished for Caleb for a new reason: for Cassie and Elaine. To provide the support they both needed, especially Elaine.

Because Devlin felt utterly inadequate in this situation.

Zoe and Kalina sat around the small fire with other UFO hunters, eating small meat rolls from a tin and canned green beans.

"We need to be somewhere else," Kalina murmured to her sister, although she doubted anyone else was listening to them as the rest chatted noisily about past sightings and future hopes.

Hope, Zoe thought sourly. What did they know of hope? Pointless lights in the sky? Stupid people. Life was too easy for them. She looked at Kalina and saw at least some of her feelings reflected there.

"Niko," Kalina said, then looked down at the tin in her hand. "He would like these little sausages."

Zoe nodded her agreement and ate another one. "Majka made the best sausage."

But their mother was no longer with them. Too many people were no longer with them. Maybe that was what had driven their brother. Too many dead and a threat that wouldn't go away. But why had he thought the Americans would help? They did little enough, leaving it to the blue-hatted peacekeepers from the UN.

Who were little use at any time.

But Niko had never spoken about his choice or why he had made the decision. Never a word to anyone, which meant the Americans must be at fault for his exposure. His activities had been revealed only when he was discovered.

And the only American who could be blamed was the one Niko had spoken to.

The young women looked at each other, their faces perplexed and tired. They needed more information than they had been given. No way to identify this devil except…except how? Every man here seemed big. Or at least, most of them did.

"We have to go," Zoe said after a few minutes. "Back to town. We'll never find him here unless he's with this group."

A man who could not possibly be perverting anyone like Niko out here. Or anywhere at all in his own country.

But if he suspected he was being hunted, their task would become harder.

Kalina agreed. How were they ever going to identify this man?

Because now they had to be as careful as Niko had been for so long.

ELAINE WORKED THAT AFTERNOON. Devlin chose to spend time with his mother and Cassie.

"It's been too long," Lu said, for what must have been the fiftieth time since he'd arrived.

And he repeated, "I'm sorry. Work. I won't let it keep me away as long as it did before."

As if he had any choice about the matter. But he could certainly try. Over the years, there'd been an increase in his ranking, and thus his authority. But with both came greater responsibilities.

Cassie had once again returned to her coloring. Kittie now sat on her lap, and Cassie reached down occasionally to pet her gently. Gentleness seemed to be part of the child.

"Mom? Does Cassie enjoy anything else? Besides coloring, I mean."

"And the kitten," Lu said dryly. "Yeah. She likes walks. We go down by the park often, but she only watches. No interest in the equipment or other children. But Sally believes that will start to change with time. We hope so."

Devlin nodded, trying to imagine how Cassie might view the world and failing miserably.

"We try to introduce her to new things, but slowly," Lu said. "See what interests her and what she doesn't like."

"This must be hard on Elaine."

"Harder than hard," Lu said. "I don't think she ever

stops sweating it, except maybe when something big happens at work."

"I could see that." Then he reached across the table and touched his mother's hand. "What about you? This can't be easy for you, either."

Lu simply shook her head. "I'd do anything for that child. And I *do* have a life, Devlin. Friends. Places I go. It's not like I'm locked up." She pursed her lips, looking faintly amused. "I'm pretty happy with my life, if you're worried about that."

It wasn't something he'd worried about much, except for a period after his father died. But Caleb had been there.

Devil stared at the curly blond hair of his totally absorbed niece and thought about how selfish he'd been. His job was important, yeah. Essential, even. But did it really leave him no time at all?

Not much of it, but that could just be an excuse.

Hell, he thought. *What have I become?*

"I'd like to walk into town," he said. A walk to clear his head. "I don't suppose Cassie would come with me?"

Lu shook her head. "Not likely. Not yet. But go ahead and ask her."

About time he seriously talked to the girl beyond a simple greeting. "Cassie? Would you like to go for a walk with me?"

The child looked up, her hand tightening slightly on Kittie's fur. The look on her face said it all.

"I guess not," Devlin said. "Maybe another time."

Lu tipped her head. "Gotta go back for a look at those loonies, huh?"

Devlin had to laugh, even though she was right. Instincts, honed by long years, drove him to want to understand what made that crowd tick. "Anything you need while I'm out? Like dinner from Maude's?"

Lu laughed. "I won't say no. Just make sure there's some salad with it."

At least the current crop of partiers downtown seemed to be spending money locally, Devlin noticed as he approached the fringes, this time without his alien mask. A few merchants had set up small kiosks outside their stores to sell kitschy items and, like at Maude's, to sell coffee and tea with a visible menu of other quick foods.

The town was adapting to the invasion pretty quickly, Devlin thought. Making the best of it since they were stuck with it. He wondered how long it would be before the invaders moved on.

Not long, he hoped, for the sake of the people who actually lived here.

He slipped into the crowd, though, aware that deputies had formed a very loose cordon to prevent any trouble that might arise.

A number of beers went down throats, but at least the drinkers used the trash bins that seemed to have sprung up along the street, avoiding littering except for scraps of paper. More preparedness.

In all, he was pretty impressed with the general behavior on both sides of this divide.

But as he threaded himself into the crowd and tuned his ears to picking out individual words that might be of interest, he learned something about why this crowd was here: Roswell had become an expensive place to go. These people needed a cheaper place to gather.

Well, that meant certain sacrifices, as he overheard. Sleeping just outside of town in their vehicles because the single motel was overflowing. He also heard the beginnings of rumbles about leaving. Moving on. Maybe finding a better place.

Except for the red lights. The lights visible from the Bixby ranch seemed to have them stapled right here. Not that they expected to see anything from town, but because they hoped they'd be the first to hear the news from the serious hunters who camped out there.

A couple of red lights, for Pete's sake. By Bixby's report, they didn't even seem to move much, if at all. But where were they? If they'd been warning lights on a cell tower for air traffic, everyone should know that, shouldn't they?

His own curiosity was definitely growing. Everything had an explanation, one that didn't involve aliens.

So he did what he did on his job. He fell into conversation with one of them, a guy who wore no mask, just some bobbing green antenna on his head.

"What do you think those lights are?" he asked.

"UFOs," the guy answered promptly. "No reason for them to be there, not as far as we know."

The woman beside him disagreed. She wore the mask with the huge dark eyes, now pushed up on her forehead so she could see. "Sheesh, Jeff, we don't know *what* they are."

Jeff shook his head. "Never gonna know if we don't try to find out. And don't forget the Roswell crash."

"That *was* weird," the woman agreed. "Two different stories within forty-eight hours. Like it was and it wasn't. But whatever it is, I don't trust the government on this."

Devlin spoke. "It's hard, huh?"

"Really hard," Jeff agreed. "Always a pile of bull. At least now they're admitting they can't explain some of this stuff. That's a big step forward."

Devlin thought it was, too. He'd been interested in that UAP report himself. More intelligence. A reason to start looking at what might be a threat to the safety of the nation. A big reason not to dismiss the sightings and reports. His entire adult life had been devoted to the security of this nation, and now this was part of it.

He couldn't criticize these people for wanting to know. Not after they'd been dismissed as fools for seventy or more years.

"Ever seen one?" he asked Jeff, to keep the conversation going. To give himself a visible excuse to keep scanning the crowd.

"A UFO?" Jeff said. "Yeah. Really. Not the kind that makes headlines or anything like that. But I saw a plane, taking off at night, suddenly split into three pieces—red light going to the left, green light going to the right and white light continuing the climb. I thought it was gonna crash."

Devlin nodded, interested. "Did it?"

"Hell no. And when the paper arrived the next afternoon, I discovered I wasn't nuts. Over four thousand people in my area had seen it, too, and called in wanting to know what it was."

"That's a lot of people."

Jeff nodded, his fuzzy green antennae bobbing above his head. "But useless as a sighting."

"So these red lights won't be useful, either?"

Jeff laughed. "Probably not. Unless someone gets some good film of them performing aerobatics that are impossible for current technology. And who knows what current technology is, anyway?"

Devlin faced him. "Then what are you doing here?"

"It's fun. A great vacation. Spring break." Then Jeff

moved away to rejoin the woman, who'd drifted into the crowd.

Spring break, huh? Devlin started grinning himself. But he suspected Jeff's curiosity was strong after what he'd seen that time before. More than a spring trip.

Being faced with the unknown, something with no explanation, could make people devote their entire lives to seeking an answer.

He wondered how many people here were driven by the same unquenchable curiosity and how many had simply found a good reason to party. Lots of things like this pulled people together for good times.

He had just started walking back toward Elaine's house, crossing a residential street not far from downtown, when he heard an irritated man's voice say, "When are those jerks ever gonna leave? Blocking the street, dressed like they ought to be locked up, making life hell for everyone who lives here."

Devlin had no problem understanding the guy's point of view. But then, that kind of understanding had aided him for years.

He paused. The man sat on his front porch on a webbed lawn chair, a longneck in his hand. A birdlike woman, probably his wife, sat in a matching chair. She held no beverage.

Taking a step closer, but not too close, he said, "My name's Devlin. I'm staying with Elaine Paltier. Lu's my mother. You know them?"

The man nodded, as did his wife. "Good people," he said. "So, you finally come home, huh? Must make Lu happy. That child sure got problems, though."

His wife spoke. "Milt, don't be unkind."

He scowled. "I ain't being unkind. That child has problems. Damn shame. Anyhow, I'm more worried about these fruitcakes out there. Looks like a fire ready for a match. There's what? A hundred of 'em?"

A hundred was probably on the conservative side, but Devlin didn't say so. "Just a bunch of kids," he remarked.

"Kids get up to no good easy enough. Bet they got drugs out there." He shook his head. "Folks are getting mighty tired of them."

"Are they?" Devlin smiled and shook his head. "I thought people were being welcoming. At least from what I see."

"That welcome's gonna wear out," Milt said. "Mark my words. Business is all tied up in knots, people can't get to the simplest things. Hell, they got Freitag's department store blocked off."

True. Devlin couldn't argue that. "Well, it's got to end soon," he remarked. "They'll get bored. It's not like this town is set up for them, not like Roswell."

Milt snorted. "Never wanted to be like that place."

His wife spoke. "Bet Roswell makes money on it, though."

"There's more to life than making money."

Devlin had to conceal his amusement, as the woman very much looked like a little more money would be welcome in her life.

After another few casual words, he bade them farewell and moved on.

How many storekeepers were starting to get truly angry, despite the attempts from some of them to take advantage of the invasion? What he had viewed as friendly only a short time ago could take on a different character quite rapidly.

He'd seen it happen.

Then that sense of threat touched him again. Nothing in particular. No sense of being watched. Just something in the air like a faint breeze.

What the hell was going on?

Chapter Eight

Elaine returned from her shift for an evening with her family and arrived to find Devlin cleaning the litter box in the bathroom and Cassie standing nearby, watching intently.

All the while, Devlin spoke quietly about what he was doing and why. Kittie stayed close to Cassie's leg, seeming almost as absorbed in the process as Cassie.

Another step? Another interest? How long would it last?

Cassie turned her head, smiled and said, "Mommy," then returned to watching the litter box cleaning.

"I'm glad," Devlin said, "that Mike Windwalker gave us the dust-free litter. I hate to imagine the cloud otherwise."

Certainly something Elaine wouldn't want Cassie breathing.

As soon as the box was cleaned and the cover back in place, Kittie decided to inaugurate it, which made a tiny laugh escape Cassie. Miracle indeed.

Lu called from the kitchen. "Wash up, folks. I'm about to heat up dinner!"

Risking it, Elaine touched Cassie's shoulder quickly, lightly. Before Cassie could pull away or otherwise react, she headed for her bedroom to ditch her uniform.

Little bits of hope, like that quick touch, every single one as welcome as a miracle.

As soon as she had changed, she found that Cassie had already made her way to the kitchen table, awaiting her dinner with Kittie on her lap.

Devlin had seated himself at the far end of the table and started to rise when Elaine entered the room. God, she'd thought those manners had died years ago. Unnecessary, too, as far as she was concerned, but it was hardly something to turn into an issue.

Lu had already moved place settings and serving dishes to the table, and mouthwatering aromas filled the air.

"It all smells too good," Elaine said. "I think I should thank you, Devlin?"

"Absolutely," Lu said. "I didn't exactly waste my time in raising him."

Devlin laughed. "No, Mom, you didn't."

Cassie continued to pet Kittie but simply stared at the food on her plate.

After a minute or so, Elaine asked, "Aren't you hungry, sweetie? I see french fries and salad. You usually like them both."

But Cassie continued to stare without eating until Elaine began to wonder if her daughter was ill. "Upset tummy, Cassie?" Sometimes that got a nod. God, it was frustrating to have a nonverbal child. Sally felt that would ease with time, that speaking later in childhood wasn't uncommon for autistic children. In the meantime, Elaine spent a whole lot of time wondering about matters such as whether Cassie was ill.

But after what seemed entirely too long, Cassie reached for a cherry tomato, lifting it with delicate fingers to pop it into her mouth.

Elaine released a breath she hadn't realized she was holding and looked away to find Devlin staring at her with sympathy. As if he understood. Maybe he did.

"So," she said, hunting for a safe topic, "what did you learn from your expedition among the weirdos?"

He smiled, shaking his head. "That most of them are here because it's a cheaper place to party than Roswell. Not that I'm sure quite a few of them won't make it to the main event in July."

"Around the time of the supposed saucer crash?"

Devlin nodded. "It's an interesting mix of people who just want to have fun and people who want to be present if the hunters get any information at all. Like the lights moving."

Elaine ate salad and a few fries before she spoke again. To her relief, Cassie was still eating. Kittie didn't seem much interested in a piece of fry, though. Elaine wondered how far she'd get explaining that it wasn't good for a cat to eat human food.

Instead, she gave her attention to Devlin. "How did your intelligence run go otherwise?"

Lu turned her head to look at her son. "'Intelligence'? Why would you do that *here*?"

"Just taking the temperature of the crowd out there. Crowds always make me a little nervous."

"You know," Lu said, "it would be nice if someday you could tell me a little about what you've been doing that's changed you this way."

Elaine expected Devlin to ask what his mother meant by him changing, but he didn't. As if he knew he didn't need to explain. Or couldn't explain.

She kept her attention on Cassie and the kitten throughout the meal, only half paying attention to the desultory conversation between Devlin and Lu.

But Lu's question had raised some questions in her own mind. He'd been off doing something these nearly twenty years. Traveling the world, she gathered, from what little he'd said. But what kind of world traveler came home without a hundred stories to share? Descriptions of sights seen and memorable places visited? Hadn't there at least been some historic monument in all his travels?

It seemed Devlin had erased a huge chunk of his past. Or locked it in a safe that required a combination to open.

That wasn't fair, though, she thought later, as she led Cassie to her bath and bed. Not fair at all.

Devlin could probably open that past any time he wanted. Or any time he needed. Well, clearly he didn't feel the need here, and his desire to had gone only as far as collecting some intelligence from that off-the-wall crowd in town.

As she sat on the rocker beside Cassie's bed, reading a Dr. Seuss book that always brought a tiny smile to Cassie's face, Elaine thought about Devlin, about his evident heap of secrets, and decided she shouldn't trust him.

A man without a past, her husband's brother or not, had plenty to conceal.

Too bad he was so attractive.

But that was unfortunate, too. Caleb's brother. Maybe time to move on, if she felt like she was cheating. But would she be, really? She doubted Caleb would ever have wanted her to spend the rest of her life alone.

And of course, there was Cassie. She had to be extremely careful about whom she let into her daughter's life. Stories about stepfathers—mostly unfair, she supposed—still concerned her.

Cassie had slipped off into her dreams, so Elaine closed the thin book and set it on the night table. A night table that had never been allowed to hold anything but a small lamp, a tiny stuffed unicorn and the book. One of the ways Cassie was particular.

Then Elaine sat there, the room illuminated now only by a night-light, and stared into the gloom.

She didn't want to return to her living room. Didn't want to see Devlin again, not right now.

She couldn't trust him, but he was living with her.

Nice.

Especially when she acknowledged a growing desire for him. It was just an inkling, but it wouldn't go away.

DEVLIN NOTICED ELAINE'S ABSENCE, hoping that Cassie wasn't having a problem. But his mother seemed undisturbed as they sat talking over coffee. They were both the kind of people who could drink coffee right up until bedtime and still sleep without a problem.

Caleb hadn't been like that.

A sigh escaped him as he thought of his brother. They'd made lots of good memories together in their younger days, some of them that had made Gage Dalton frown. A frown you very much didn't want to be on the receiving end of.

Gage had made no secret that he thought teenage boys had no sense of judgment or consequences, and he preferred to teach those things with a frown and a good lecture. Gage possessed a scowl that would scare the willies out of you.

But he also didn't like to arrest kids or teach them a lesson overnight in one of those cells above his office. So it all depended on just how bad you were. And Gage was the judge and jury for that, unless he decided the transgression was serious enough to have Judge Wyatt Carter look down at them from his bench.

The magistrate usually handled those minor problems, but there were times when Gage determined something more was required. Thus, the judge.

Devlin grinned, and Lu caught sight of it. "What's so funny?"

"Just remembering some of the hijinks Caleb and I got up to."

Lu snorted. "Plenty of those, as I recall. You weren't very good at keeping secrets back then."

"Not with everybody from the principal to half the town willing to tattle."

Lu laughed. "Never did learn."

"Hell no. Too much fun."

Fun, he realized, was very much a thing of his past. At least the wild, cutting-loose kind of fun he and Caleb and their friends had gotten into.

Was that just growing up? Or did life change some people, like him, from the carefree idiots they'd once been?

What did it matter? He was the man he was now. Couldn't flip that overnight, nor did he think he wanted to.

Finally, Elaine emerged from Cassie's room. Her uniform had given way to jeans and a denim shirt. She'd knotted the tails around her waist, showing just a finger's width of skin. He'd always liked that look, although it was not often seen anymore. Probably because of those crop tops.

Man, was he thinking about women's fashion? He was losing it in more ways than one.

"I'm thinking," he said when it was clear that no conversation was in the offing, "of driving out and taking a look at those lights myself."

Elaine plopped down in the chair facing him. "Why? I thought we already saw them."

He shook his head. "Curiosity," he said. "It's bugging me."

"Well, nobody's apparently ever figured them out. Beggan Bixby says he's been seeing them his whole life. Near as I can tell, nobody ever paid them any mind until this lot turned up. What do you possibly think you can learn?"

"How about," he suggested, "that it's going to drive me to the edge if I can't figure something out."

Elaine laughed. "Good luck, Devlin. But tell you what, I'll ride along. Lu? Is that okay?"

Lu, holding her reader in her lap, waved them on. "Get out of here so I can read my book without red lights in the sky."

Elaine and Devlin laughed quietly as they left the house.

DEVLIN HAD RENTED a Jeep for driving out here—he apparently remembered that much about the terrain—and they took his vehicle. Elaine liked that because in his car, without her uniform, she didn't feel even remotely like she was on duty.

Although she carried her pistol on her hip. Required, even off duty. But in the Jeep, she could ignore it. No crackling radios, no computer screen flashing information, no extra dash controls and no shotgun racked upright and locked between the two front seats.

She was able to relax, to allow her head to sag back against the headrest, to allow her entire body to unwind. For a while, it was plenty to have the window cracked just enough for a chilly breeze to blow gently on her face. She just pulled her jacket closer and inhaled the fresh, sage-scented night.

"You and Caleb ever get out here?" Elaine asked a while later. "Or were you town guys?"

"We had friends who lived on the ranches out here. Plenty of long weekends, even a couple of summer camping trips. Then when we got older, we had some summer jobs."

"A broad experience, then?"

"Oh, definitely. The hard labor was good, although I'm sure we were never as good as an experienced hand could be." He snorted. "We *did* spend some work time cutting up."

"Irresistible."

"Seemed to be. But we didn't get in any trouble for it. Our friends' dads seemed to be understanding, although from time to time, they'd remind us we were *working*."

A small laugh escaped Elaine. "You were lucky."

"We sure were. Good people who made allowances for us. What about you? Townie?"

"Yeah, almost all the time. A different kind of experience, but the nice thing was that my friends were all nearby and it was easy to get together."

"You still have any of those friends?"

Again, Elaine laughed. "I've still got most of my friends but we've developed different interests. You?"

"I doubt it. Just absence. Gone. Probably forgotten by now."

Elaine nodded slowly. That was kind of sad.

"My choice," Devlin said. "They were all my choices."

But he didn't sound as if he thought that was such a

good thing. Maybe coming home had changed his perspective.

The way she had been changed by Caleb's death. The way she had been changed by the growing understanding of Cassie's problems.

Life could do that to you. A single thing could change, and nothing ever looked the same again.

ELAINE POINTED OUT to Devlin the spot along the road where she'd first seen the red whatevers that had made her think there might be a range fire.

Devlin pulled over immediately and asked her to point as best she could. "I don't see them now, though."

"Me, either. How big were they?"

"Not very. Just big enough to catch my eye and make me worry about fire."

He stirred in his seat, making the leather creak. "Did they get bigger as you approached Bixby's place?"

Elaine thought back to that night. "I think so. I know I was getting pretty wound up about the possibility of a range fire by the time I reached him. Yeah, they seemed to be getting bigger, or I wouldn't have thought the fire could be spreading."

"Okay." Another few minutes, then Devlin said, "Exactly for how long did you see them?"

"I saw them all the way to Bixby's place from here up the road to his house, and then after I left, they were visible for a short while until they winked out. All told, maybe a half hour, tops."

She could feel him looking at her.

"They winked out?"

"No better way to describe it."

"Okay, that's weird. Had to be mechanical, don't you think?"

At that, a laugh began in her belly and rolled out of her. Damn, it felt good. "You ask me if that's weird when we've got a whole bunch of green-costumed people partying in the street and a somewhat more sensible group camped out here hoping to see some *lights*?"

"Well, when you put it that way…" He started to laugh, too. "So I'm on this wild goose chase because…"

"You need a concrete answer," she finished for him. "I'd like one, too, but I'm not holding my breath. Bixby says they've been there off and on his entire life. So maybe it's the aurora. Once in a while we see it down here."

"At least the aurora would be a logical explanation."

"Yeah, I could live with that. But I don't think the aurora would make two defined spots like that."

He laughed again. "Don't crush my hopes."

They drove another mile, closer to Beggan Bixby's ranch, when Elaine suddenly said, "There!" She pointed.

Devlin wheeled the Jeep onto the shoulder without going far enough to tip them into a drainage ditch. He switched off the car and lights; then they jumped out to look.

There they were—two red lights, brighter than Elaine had recalled, and certainly bigger.

"Wow," she breathed. She hadn't expected *this*.

"It's like my mind made them smaller," he said. "It turned those two red orbs into the kind of pinpricks you'd see from the top of a cell phone tower."

"They've grown," Elaine said. "A whole lot."

"Well, that should make the UFO hunters happy."

"Yeah, but probably not Bixby. Or Lew Selvage. He said they could camp on his property."

"That group is about to grow."

Where would that lead, Elaine wondered. It wasn't as if she could just sit back and enjoy the show. She thought of calling Lew Selvage to ask how the hunters he'd allowed on his property were behaving, whether they were giving him trouble.

Then she remembered they were in a communication dead zone. Still hard to believe, even after all this time, that even a sat phone wouldn't work out here.

She guessed she'd have to wait until she got back to town.

Devlin surprised her by going to the rear of the Jeep and returning with a rather impressive pair of binoculars. "Boy, do you come prepared."

His smile was hard to see in the darkness of the night, but she caught a glimpse of it anyway.

"You got a good sporting-goods store in town. Jackson was kind enough to rent them to me."

"Well, it would be hard to get them any bigger. At least around here."

He put them to his eyes, gave them a bit of adjustment and focused toward the lights.

After a minute, she asked impatiently, "Well?"

"Two orange-ish red lights. Nothing else. Wanna look?" He started to pass the binoculars to her, but she waved them away.

"Just lights?" she asked.

"Just lights. Of course, these binoculars only see in the visible spectra. I wonder if your UFO hunters are better equipped."

"They're not *my* hunters, and you'll have to ask them."

He laughed. "Point taken. Well, as far as visible light

goes, that's all they are. Lights. But I can't figure out what they're doing there."

"I sure couldn't. Nobody seems to know, but then nobody's been paying much attention all these years. So I suggest we drive on a little farther. Maybe you'll see them wink out the way I did."

"Which will create another mystery. They shouldn't be there, but if they are, then why do they turn off? It's got to be mechanical. With some kind of timer."

Elaine had to agree with that. Nothing else made any sense.

"Devlin," she said as she thought about what they were doing, "you're so bored that you're trying to go down the rabbit hole."

He chuckled but shook his head. "I just like to solve problems. And this is the problem *du jour*."

PROBLEM OR NOT, Devlin thought as they began driving again, the main thing was enjoying this time with Elaine. Seeing her relax this way. No worries for just a couple of hours.

He just wished he didn't find her so attractive. Life would have been easier without feeling such a strong physical tug toward her. Apart from her having been Caleb's wife, which was enough to swamp him with shame if he let it, she had more important matters to occupy her. Like Cassie. Elaine couldn't seem to find much time in her life for anything but work and her daughter.

That was something he actually understood, having been guilty of something similar most of his adult life. A life he needed to remember that he'd return to, leaving nothing for anyone else behind him.

That would be cruel, even assuming Elaine wanted to

fit a new relationship into her life. Building a decent relationship took a lot of time and effort. He'd never been able to stay around long enough for most of the effort part.

For once, he cursed the skills that made him such a good covert operative. He could read people. He could assess their motivations fairly well. Judge the shortages and weaknesses in their lives.

Right now he saw an Elaine whose life was too full to make room for anything else. Apart from her job, she lived with constant emotional worry. He doubted she forgot Cassie often, even when at work.

But none of that kept him from wanting her, from wanting to feel her curves pressed against him, her warm smooth skin beneath his hands, the warm hot depths of her surrounding him.

Oh, man. Stop now.

Think of Cassie instead. He was coming to love that little girl, and experiencing the first glimmers of frustration and fear that Elaine must feel on an almost constant basis. Was that an improvement? Was it real? How much? Would it remain? Would it expand?

God. He thought of Cassie's wonderful gentleness with the kitten and decided her therapist, Sally, was brilliant for thinking of it. When he'd first met Cassie and begun to realize the extent of her problems, he'd never have thought of her being able to take care of a pet.

Yet there she was. A step to bigger things? Did it matter, when Cassie's love for the kitten was so evident?

And then it happened. A strong sense of connection with Elaine slammed into him. As if for an instant their hearts connected. A feeling so strong that he almost missed the instant when the lights in the sky winked out.

"Oh, for the love of heaven," he said in exasperation.

Growing distracted was an unfamiliar experience for him. Not one he could afford. That's what Elaine did to him.

"What?" Elaine demanded.

"I almost missed the lights winking out. And what the hell made them turn off like that?"

"Well, you saw it happen, for what that's worth."

"Yeah, but now it's too late to chase. I want to come out here tomorrow night and try to triangulate them."

Elaine erupted into a full-throated laugh. "Oh, God, Devlin, I never thought I'd see you turn into one of *them*."

She might have a point, he thought, and he joined in her laughter.

"It's different," he protested.

"Right. And Mitch has part of his pasture full of people who think there must be something *real* in those lights. People who may even be trying to triangulate them. People who think they're just a mystery to be solved."

"Dang, Elaine." But he had to laugh anyway. "Nailed it."

"I like it," she said. "Makes you seem more human."

Oh, now he needed to seem human? What the hell was he acting like? Had he become as reserved as some kind of robot?

Questions that were suddenly more important than some lights in the sky.

Who had Devlin Paltier become?

WHEN THEY REACHED the house, Lu was already sound asleep in her bed, the baby monitor on the night table near her head.

Devlin and Elaine walked quietly, trying not to disturb Lu or Cassie, and made their way to the kitchen, where Elaine decided to make some hot chocolate.

A small sound caught her attention, and she looked down to see that Kittie had abandoned Cassie's bed and was looking up with sleepy eyes.

"Aw, sweetie," she said quietly, then lifted the kitten into her arms. The cat snuggled in and began to purr. "This cat has the right idea," she remarked. "Just enjoy everything in life."

"Yeah. Good lesson. Let me make the hot chocolate."

She stepped away from the stove and took a seat at the table. "I hope Cassie doesn't wake up looking for her." That concerned her.

"I think Cassie knows her way out here. This would be the first place she'd look, don't you think?"

"Maybe." Looking down at the purring kitten in her arms, Elaine decided this was one thing she just couldn't worry about. Somehow Cassie would have to get used to the fact that the kitten couldn't spend its entire life on her lap or beside her arm at the table.

She looked at Devlin, who was stirring the cocoa. "I need to start playing with Kittie. A cat needs playtime, and maybe Cassie will pick it up."

Another hope. Always another hope, too often followed by a crash. But she let herself have those moments anyway. Every once in a while, Cassie shattered those disappointments with a big step. Like calling her *Mommy.*

And while Cassie didn't like hugs, generally didn't like to be touched, she allowed Elaine to bathe her and dress her. Even pull her covers up. Good things.

There'd be more. She had to believe it. Sally certainly thought so. And look at this lovely kitten. A huge step, a beautiful one.

She smiled as Devlin placed a mug of hot chocolate in front of her. Kittie chose that moment to jump down and head out of the kitchen door, her tail raised high like a flag with a crook at the very top.

"I guess she's claimed her home here," Devlin remarked. "At least, I've heard that about cats' tails."

"Me, too."

A minute later, they heard scratching from the area of the cat box. When Kittie didn't reappear, Elaine assumed she'd returned to bed with Cassie. At least, she hoped she had. She didn't want to imagine Cassie's upset if the cat was gone in the morning.

Because Cassie, who appeared to be a placid child with serious limits on how she could be treated, was capable of having memorable meltdowns when seriously bothered. The worst part of those meltdowns for Elaine was that she couldn't, and never had, found a way to calm Cassie. Those spells just had to burn themselves out.

They were based entirely in sensory overload, though, and sometimes there was just no way to predict where an overload could come from. Looking for Kittie and not finding her might spark one.

Elaine, however, resisted the urge to go make sure Kittie had returned to Cassie's bed. As far as she knew, it was hard to make a cat do anything it didn't want to do.

DEVLIN WATCHED THE play of emotions over Elaine's face and wished he could help. But how? Cassie was, justifiably, the center of Elaine's life, and nothing was going to change that. Not now, not ever. Nor should it.

He looked down at the cooling mug of cocoa in front of him so that she wouldn't feel like she was being stared at, even though he was getting to the point where he never wanted to look away.

A bad place to be, when he had nothing to offer and a

job that would take him away again. A month? Was that all he had to offer?

He stifled a sigh and tried not to analyze himself too hard. He had always believed in what he was doing, the importance of it.

Now he was looking at something that in its own way could be every bit as important. The job had also twisted him in ways he didn't want to think about. When lying came as easily as breathing when you needed it, what did that make a person?

That he could still tell the difference was probably his only saving grace.

Elaine rose, dumping her remaining cocoa in the sink. "I have an early morning, so I'll turn in."

He watched her go and had the worst feeling that her absence was cutting a hole in him.

Then he told himself not to be ridiculous. People came and went from his life. That was the nature of the beast.

He had a couple of friends, colleagues who had become more than people he just worked with. But only a couple. Getting too close was dangerous in his line of work.

It could also be dangerous to Elaine, he reminded himself. Not just over a few weeks, but if the relationship extended longer? If she became more important to him?

There might also be a danger to Lu and Cassie.

Given his recent experience with Niko, he didn't exactly trust all his coworkers. Someone had talked. What if they learned enough to talk about his family?

Another week. He'd get out of here soon.

ELAINE COULDN'T HELP HERSELF. She peeked into Cassie's bedroom, the door never closed all the way, and saw Kittie curled up once again on the bed, near Cassie's head. For now, that was okay.

But after she finished her shower and climbed into her flannel pajamas, she stretched out on her bed and didn't sleep.

Sleep eluded her primarily because she couldn't stop thinking about Devlin. Sadly enough, she knew his visit was short. His job had kept him away for years and absolutely no reason to think that might change.

She also had a strong suspicion embassy duties barely covered what he was up to. Having to get away? Having to go to the ends of the earth for a "vacation"? She wasn't buying it. There were other things, too. Hints.

Even so. She rolled over and hugged her pillow, wishing it were Devlin. Silly, she told herself. Attraction to a man who'd be gone so soon? Her husband's brother?

Yet that guilt didn't plague her as much as she would have expected. Caleb and Devlin were different in so many ways. Maybe because they'd spent the last years so far apart, pursuing such different jobs. It wasn't as if she were attracted to Caleb's clone.

Yeah, that would explain it.

But a pillow, even a firm body pillow, couldn't make the bed less empty. Couldn't replace the warmth of Caleb's muscular body beside hers. How she had teased him about being a heat engine. The way she could tuck her feet between his legs and they'd never get cold.

That had always amused Caleb, but he'd never once complained. He'd retorted that she was his summer air conditioner, so it was all fair.

Except it wasn't fair that he wasn't there right now. Even after two years, she felt the emptiness in that big bed. Often thought of exchanging it for a smaller one so maybe it wouldn't feel so empty.

But she couldn't let go of the bed she and Caleb had chosen together. It was nothing fancy because it'd had to fit their budget, but it had a wooden carved headboard. No footboard because Caleb was too tall and would have shoved it away and broken the bed. Not that Elaine cared about a footboard.

She cared about little in this room except the way it made her stomach feel hollow.

At last, sleep slipping away and coming no closer, she pulled on her gray robe, pulled her hair into a ponytail and headed for the kitchen. It was the one room in the house where if she made a little noise, it wouldn't be heard in all the bedrooms.

To her surprise, she found Devlin sitting there with what smelled like fresh coffee. He wore a chambray shirt that stretched across his broad shoulders, jeans and a pair of socks. His dark hair was tousled.

"Can't sleep?" he asked.

"No. What about you?"

"Way different time zone. I'm still trying to adjust."

Way different from where? Certainly farther than the East Coast, if he was still adjusting.

"Fresh coffee," he said, pointing with his mug. "Unless it'll keep you awake even more."

"I'm one of the lucky ones. Doesn't do that to me."

She sat facing him, then looked down at her coffee and the table, unable to think of a thing to say. Although, at this time of night, maybe conversation wasn't necessary.

Devlin didn't seem to think so. Except for the faint occasional sound of his sips and the cup coming to rest on the table, he might not have been there.

Then Kittie arrived, jumping up on the table with amazing grace. Devlin reached out to pet her gently. Kittie rubbed her head against his palm and began to purr.

"You wouldn't think," Elaine said, "that such a small cat could purr so loudly."

"Kind of amazing," he agreed. "But I shouldn't pet her. She needs to attach to Cassie, not to me."

"You may be right." Which didn't make the kitten any easier to resist. Still, Devlin dropped his hand, leaving it on the table. Kittie rubbed against it a couple of times; then, evidently realizing it wasn't going to rub back, she jumped down and disappeared.

Another cup of coffee later, with sleep still stubbornly eluding Elaine, he spoke again. "Is Gage getting uneasy about the green party with the bouncy eyes?"

She snorted. "Probably, but he's not saying anything. Yet."

"All that drinking in the streets. I'm not used to it."

That might have revealed more than he realized, Elaine thought. Had he been somewhere alcohol wasn't allowed?

Then he half dashed her speculation. "Funny, I don't remember open-container being legal here. It's not most other places."

"It's always been legal here in public spaces. Better not drive under the influence, though. Or operate a vehicle with an open container that's in reach of the driver. There *are* limits."

He nodded and leaned back in his chair. "That party could turn into mayhem easily enough. Put enough beer in 'em and look out."

"That's always a risk. We're forever having to break up brawls at Mahoney's or one of the roadhouses out in the county. Most excitement we usually get around here." Thank God.

"Not always, though?"

"Not always." She shook her head, simply not wanting to talk about the downsides of her job. Of course worse things than drunken brawls happened. People lived here, and people weren't perfect. Everything from spousal abuse to the occasional murder happened around here. Even one kidnapping.

Which, as the previous sheriff would have groused, meant the county was going to hell in a handbasket. Elaine had always loved that phrase but doubted it was true. More likely an expression of frustration when things *did* go wrong.

Her cell phone buzzed suddenly, and a quick glance at the screen told her it was the office. Kind of them not to set off the much louder satellite phone.

She picked it up. "Paltier." Then she listened a moment, and said, "You've got to be kidding me! I'll be there."

She jumped up, heading for her bedroom and her uniform. Before she got out the kitchen door to head for the hallway, Devlin's voice halted her briefly. "What's wrong?"

"Cattle mutilation," she said between her teeth. "And I'm sure it didn't involve any little green men!"

Chapter Nine

Elaine didn't argue when Devlin climbed into her Suburban beside her. She was past arguing about anything. She was exhausted from lack of sleep, seriously bothered that she'd had to wake Lu to tell her she was going on duty. Worse, she was frankly furious that she'd miss breakfast with Cassie, something she tried strenuously never to do.

A mutilated cow? Seriously? She'd heard about such things but was inclined to believe they were some kind of misdiagnosed predation. Especially since it was her understanding that veterinarians didn't even want to look at a "mutilated" carcass anymore.

"Cattle mutilation?" Devlin said as they raced through the night. "I thought that had been debunked."

"It has been. I heard a few ranchers lost a lot of cattle somewhere or other, and in a case or two they lost their entire ranches because of it, but if it were me, I'd be getting all my neighbors together to start hunting for big cats. Bobcats. Cougars. Whatever."

"Aren't they leaving meat behind, or something?"

She shook her head. "I don't know. I gather, in these cases, they leave a lot behind, which I would think is unusual, but big cats wouldn't be the first animals that took to killing just because they like it. Packs of wild dogs will do that."

"Like *us*," he remarked.

She nearly snorted. "Too much so, sometimes."

He fell silent as the miles sped away, often with the sound of gravel hitting the rear of her vehicle. His silence was fine, although she was a little surprised that he had so much knowledge about cattle mutilations tucked away.

What the hell did he do for a living?

"Now," she muttered as she turned onto Mitch Cantrell's road. The man was a wealthy cattle rancher who also took care of a large flock of sheep for his bride, Grace. He could withstand the loss of one or two head of cattle, but he'd still be furious. Maybe want to toss those nuts off his land.

She shook her head, thinking about the mess. They'd have to figure out who'd killed the cow and made it look like a mutilation, if it even really was. Well, obviously a suspect could come from the UFO crowd, who stood to gain from such a story. Which wasn't a good thing, given those fools were hanging around all over the place now, annoying the locals. More people than Mitch were going to be angry about this.

So they had this crowd they'd have to both protect and get out of town while hunting for whoever had pulled this ugly stunt. Because she seriously doubted one person could do this. Damn calf was probably pushing six hundred pounds, if not more.

Poison, maybe? Well, the state lab could check for that. Among a million other things, she supposed.

As they drove up Cantrell's road, her hands tightened on her steering wheel until they ached. At the ranch house, one of Mitch's cowboys was waiting for them. "Out that way," he said, pointing with a powerful flashlight. "You won't get far before you'll see a whole bunch of these lights. You won't see any of your own floodlights out there yet. I suppose they're coming."

"I'm sure they'll come. How's the crowd?"

The cowboy shook his head. "We been keeping an eye on 'em. They didn't get anywhere near that damn calf, not since one of 'em found it. Tripped on it, actually. Kid was screaming his fool head off."

Elaine thanked him and rolled up her window. "Well, hot damn," she said irritably. "This is going to be fun."

Devlin didn't say a word.

ZOE AND KALINA knew they had to get away the instant one of the ranch guys watching the group had started cussing about a dead cow.

The ranch hands who watched the group had changed out during the day, but always at least two of them kept an eye on the group.

Come sunset, the telescopes and cameras always got set up. A couple of those telescopes watched all day, but as far as Kalina and Zoe could tell, they never saw anything. Or at least, no one let on to any excitement.

But then those lights at night. The two women admitted to each other that the sight of the lights unnerved them. Not rockets. Not helicopters, not even the threatening drones that had hovered over their people too often. Just red lights hanging there, almost like a demon's eyes.

Children of their own culture, demons were part of the lore they had learned while growing up. They were just stories for children, of course, but some of their elders had nonetheless believed them, and Zoe and Kalina couldn't quite shake them.

They slipped down into a drainage ditch, easing themselves away from the crowd that had provided protection, and leaned back against the side, ignoring the prickly dry grass.

"We've got to leave," Kalina said.

"Yes. That man is going to make noise about the cow, and others will come." It was not like at home, where people who raised livestock had no way to complain if some were killed.

"Police. I don't want to talk to police."

Neither did Zoe. She knew she and her sister had unmistakable accents and while these bizarre skywatchers might not notice or care, neither of the women trusted police to ignore it. They knew too much about police, none of it good.

In fact, they were terrified of just about anyone in uniforms of any kind. With good reason.

They huddled together against the deepening chill of the spring night and listened as the crowds grew, as the huge lights pierced the night. Their shadowed space seemed to shrink. The pistol was nestled in one of Zoe's pockets, while additional bullets were in another. A small bottle of poison filled a space in Kalina's pocket. They never talked about the instruments of death. As if they didn't exist. Until tonight.

Now they knew they'd made a mistake poisoning that cow. Yes, it had been a distraction. Yes, the cow had started to die elsewhere, leaving most of its blood behind before it got here. Informative for their possible future plan. But it had drawn too much attention, and the small dogs that had torn at it briefly after it fell had only made it worse, judging by the excited conversation around them.

"We shouldn't have been sent," Kalina said suddenly,

although quietly. "There are others better suited than us." Others who wouldn't make such foolish mistakes.

"But it was explained to us," Zoe said. "Most people don't expect women to come seeking vengeance."

"Perhaps in this part of the world." Kalina shook her head, now unable to accept the whole idea of this mission. In her heart of hearts, she believed Niko wouldn't want his sisters taking on this risk. He had tried so hard to protect his family.

She also knew that she had agreed to carry vengeance across the world. The poison had worked on the cow, she reassured herself. It would work on the man, too. But they still hadn't found a way to get close enough to give him the poison. Or even shoot him.

They had begun to think they knew who he was, though. A local man who'd surprised the town by returning recently.

Still, she and her sister weren't the best choice for this job.

But family honor needed to be avenged, too. Niko had been an informant, had possibly betrayed his own people.

Neither Zoe nor Kalina truly believed he would have betrayed them or their parents, or even his friends. If he was passing information, it must have been about the other side.

But they had no proof. Judgment on Niko had been rendered, and he had died. All that was left was vengeance.

And two Eastern European women were far less likely to draw attention in this country than two men.

Not that there was a lot to choose between men's and women's roles anymore. Not with endless war. Sooner or later, everyone became a combatant.

But thinking about this whole situation wasn't helping

them complete their mission. They had to find a way back to town for a longer time than the few short trips they'd taken with members of this group. Into town, where it was likelier they could reach their target.

And those red lights kept staring balefully at them.

ELAINE AND DEVLIN hadn't arrived much sooner than the crime scene unit. It wasn't the biggest unit, Devlin noticed. Probably didn't have much call for them around here.

But there was no mistaking the mutilated calf lying on the ground. Elaine's estimate of six hundred pounds might have been on the low side.

The first thing he noticed was lack of visible blood. Now, you couldn't just butcher an animal this size and have no blood. There should have been at least some on the hide around the wounds. He could envision most of it soaking away or staying inside the animal, but...

It was a head-scratcher, one he would have to think about. Everything had a reason.

"Damn," said one deputy, a young guy with glasses. "That's what those folks talk about! No blood!"

"Easy," said an older deputy with long gray hair. Micah Parish, Devlin seemed to recall. A Cherokee who'd caused some ripples in this town when he arrived, a place that was probably still not very friendly to Indigenous people. They'd sure eventually made an exception for Micah, though, and a few others.

"Easy?" the young man said, his voice rising. "Tell me where the blood is."

Micah's jaw set. "Where are you expecting to find it, son? That calf's been lying on the ground for a while. It's night. It could have all soaked into the earth right there under the animal, and we wouldn't see it. There's probably a whole lot of it inside that calf. Now, calm down or go back to the office. We don't need panic."

"But the cuts…" The young man trailed off as Micah turned to face him directly.

"Back to the office," Micah said flatly. "Don't make me tell you again."

The youngster skedaddled. Micah returned his attention to the calf, and Elaine went to stand beside him. Devlin wasn't far behind.

"Luminol," Elaine said.

Devlin was familiar with the substance and how it made blood glow under UV light. "Too soon?" he asked.

Elaine glanced at him. "Definitely too soon. The techs need to finish their other tasks." She looked at Micah. "What do you think? Back everyone away behind a cordon?"

"Yeah, we don't need a lot of chin-wagging, and there's been enough trampling by us guys. Tell Sampson to get the tape up. Then choose four people to go interview that group over there. The hired hands who were watching them say none of them went near that calf."

He rocked on his heels.

"But someone did," Elaine remarked.

"Hell yeah," Devlin agreed. "Diversion."

Both Micah and Elaine looked at him. "Diversion from what?" Micah asked.

"Damned if I know. But it's so out of place it's like a neon sign in the middle of a dark, empty road."

"Well, hell," Micah said, and squatted beside the carcass, now awash in the growing number of floodlights. "Well, hell."

THE CORDONED-OFF area and brilliant lights didn't draw a crowd, thank goodness. Too far out on ranchland to get any lookie-loos at this time of night. Remaining were the crime scene unit along with six deputies, two ranch hands, an annoyed Mitch Cantrell and a huddled group of UFO hunters who weren't even pretending to watch those lights in the sky.

Then, at last, after a million photographs and some poking and prodding from the coroner, the luminol was sprayed in a wide area. The UV light turned on.

And almost nothing glowed.

Silence fell, no one making a single sound. No one moving.

Finally, Elaine whispered, "Impossible." She looked at Devlin and saw that his face had hardened into a granite frown.

"Nothing's impossible," he said roughly. *"Nothing."*

But like the rest of them, he felt as if he stood there looking at the impossible.

SOME OF THE UFO hunters had lost their taste for being out on the empty land in the dead of night after the cow's death, and climbed into their cars as soon as they were allowed to leave. Kalina and Zoe managed to hitch a ride with two of the guys.

The men were talking excitedly about the dead cow, their voices loud with adrenaline as they pored over every idea they'd ever heard about mutilations and talked about official positions and ever more about cover-ups.

"We saw it, dude!" said the passenger in the front seat. "We *saw* it. Not just a picture in a book or on TV, but the real thing. And we never saw nothing come near it. Not even a helicopter!"

"Yeah." The driver was slightly less excited, his mind apparently already moving ahead. "How do you think they'll explain it away? They always do, don't they?"

At that, the passenger fell silent. Zoe and Kalina exchanged looks, suspecting that the excitement in the front seat was slowly calming into something else. Maybe something darker.

"They can't hide all those pictures they took out there," the passenger said.

"Wanna bet? They got full control of them. They can bury them and replace them with something else. How you gonna prove it?"

Sadly, Zoe and Kalina were used to seeing things that had no rational explanation, at least to their minds. Things that were often covered up with amazing speed until you thought you'd imagined all the horror. But this time there was a rational explanation. Neither allowed themselves to even think about it.

Was believing something was imagined any better than knowing it was real? The young women had decided that, although they sometimes talked about it, testing one sister's sanity against the other's.

Now they listened to these young men talk about the very same questions that had plagued them for years. Was it real? Would it be hidden?

"Maybe we should have stayed," said the driver. "So they couldn't hide anything."

"What good would that do?" his passenger scoffed. "They've published photographs of mutilations for years and almost nobody believes it anyway. Veterinarians don't even believe it."

"They're part of the conspiracy," said the driver. "They'd lose their licenses if they told the truth."

"Well, I say we go back tomorrow by daylight and see if we can get our *own* photos."

The driver remained silent. In gratitude, Zoe and Kalina soaked up the car's interior heat and fell asleep for the rest of the drive.

Their nightmares followed them, as always.

AT THE RANCH, HOWEVER, little had quieted. Mitch Cantrell, a levelheaded man, had left his anger behind and now studied the remains along with the crime scene folks, the coroner and the remaining cops.

"It's a puzzle," Mitch said eventually. "Honestly never seen a cow dead like this. Usually predators do a good job of cleaning it up, leaving bits for smaller hunters. This was a wasteful kill."

He walked over to stand by Gage Dalton, who'd arrived fifteen minutes ago. "Maybe those UFO guys scared a predator off."

"Or they did it," Gage said. "If that calf needed moving from the kill site, it'd have taken more than one man to do it." He looked at Elaine. "What do you think?"

"How should I know? I'm not a ranch girl. But as for the UFO hunters scaring something off..." She shrugged. "If that group was scary enough to do that, then a predator wouldn't have come round, would he?"

Devlin eyed her, one corner of his mouth lifting. "What are you suggesting? Little green men?"

He was glad to hear her laugh. "Of course not. It's a puzzle, like Mitch said, but we'll get to the bottom of it."

Mitch pointed. "Something had to drag that calf here. Be easier to tell in the morning light."

Eventually a big truck pulled in, and a backhoe lifted the cow into the bed.

The evidence was carted away for a necropsy.

Elaine stared at the ground, troubled.

Devlin looked at Mitch. "You gonna hunt?"

"Believe it," Mitch said. "A bobcat. A pack of wolves...
Yeah, we're gonna hunt, starting at dawn. But it's still
weird." Then he looked over his shoulder. "It's kinda obvious to me that those two guys couldn't have been keeping watch like they were supposed to, or this couldn't have
happened. Somebody's lying about something."

Devlin nodded. "Never saw so many remains left behind, though."

"Or so little blood." But then Mitch laughed. "Well,
this'll fuel the party in town."

"Don't remind me," Gage groused.

Elaine looked at him. "You mean you're not enjoying
the invasion?"

Gage scowled at her, then grinned. "It sure as hell is
different. Nothing like it in this county's entire history."

Gage was right. Despite the area's long history, some
of it quite violent, this was still a first, all right.

"But it's probably wild animals," Elaine remarked without preamble as she and Devlin drove back into town.

"Had to be." But his suspicions ran in a different direction. The killing had been achieved with those UFO
hunters nearby. That didn't sound like animals at all. At-
tacked animals screamed or made some kind of noise, no
matter how silent a predator might be. Someone should
have heard something if that calf had died right there.

No, his thoughts ran to poison. But then, who had cut
the animal like that? Someone must have moved it there.
Sure as hell someone should have seen something.

At home, Elaine confessed her exhaustion, and without any apology, she headed for her bed. Cassie and Lu
still slept, leaving Devlin in a silent house, which he

kept mostly darkened. A pot of coffee was his only self-indulgence.

Plenty to think about, and he didn't see any good purpose in entirely adjusting his biological rhythm to Wyoming. He'd be headed back out into the field somewhere soon enough. Somewhere the time difference would be large enough to require adjustment again. The less adjustment, the better. He preferred to have a clear mind, not a sleep-fogged one, no matter where in the world he was, no matter the kind of assignment.

Although this time he figured they'd keep him low-visibility, with few demands. At least for a while.

And he'd sure love to know who had squealed about Niko. He didn't care if it had been inadvertent, because it had cost Niko his life, and Devlin feared that the dominoes of that revelation hadn't yet quit tumbling. Not only was he at risk, but his entire circle of assets might now be at risk, too.

Ripples. Always ripples. Pretty on a pond, hellish in real life.

Despite his other concerns, he had plenty of time in the predawn darkness to think about Elaine, Cassie, his mother. About a dead calf that needed some explaining.

He slapped a salami sandwich together, remembering only at the last moment to squirt it with some mustard. Then, sitting at the table again with fresh coffee, he ruminated, turning things around in his mind in whatever order they showed up. That mental Ferris wheel had always served him well, moving, moving, moving until bits and pieces started to make sense. Sometimes giving him a bird's-eye view of his own rambling thoughts.

Until, little by little, the randomness would begin to

yield a bit of order, like a thousand-piece puzzle without a picture on the box to guide him.

Some colors would grow brighter. Others would fade a bit. All of them mattered, but how they meshed was the important first step or two.

But tonight his thoughts weren't handing him much as a guide. The dead calf really troubled him. A threat? A strange place to make one, so far away from anything. Yet the lack of blood couldn't be accidental. How could either an animal or a human have killed and mutilated that cow while no one noticed?

Mitch was right: that calf had to have been dragged there. Without anyone from that UFO group noticing a thing? Hell, not even one of those aliens could manage that. Just think of the Travis Walton story. A bunch of his friends had seen him disappear into a beam of light. No, every UFO story he could think of had been witnessed somehow, or there'd have been no story to tell. Except the supposed mutilations, which made them even more problematic.

Not that he was any expert. A boundless curiosity led him to dip into a bunch of things, but not necessarily deeply. Aliens and UFOs had never seemed like something worth a whole lot of his time, even with the AATIP report from the Pentagon that said some of the sightings couldn't be explained.

Well, a whole lot of things in life would never be explained.

But Devlin liked finding explanations, and that damn calf sure deserved one. Especially considering the people who had descended on this town. Odd to have a cattle mutilation when all these weirdos had turned up for a party and to watch a couple of lights in the sky. So far, he'd found the costumed group in town to be amusing. No real trouble, just a group having a lot of fun among themselves. He found it hard to believe that any of them would have killed and mutilated a calf for entertainment or excitement. Although he knew people well enough to realize that they could astonish him.

He had to admit, the lights troubled him, the way no one knew what they were and all the years they'd been there. Until the past few days, no one had seen them move. But they didn't trouble Devlin enough to spend countless nights out there trying to get some tidbit of information about them.

They certainly didn't occupy his thoughts the way Elaine, Cassie and Lu did. He'd gone from being a man without a family to one who very definitely had a family. Ready made. All he'd needed to do was step into the waiting shoes.

An act that was beginning to prove remarkably easy. Even his guilt over Elaine being his brother's wife seemed to be fading.

But what wasn't fading was the idea that he'd have to leave for long spells, maybe years at a time, and he might well be in danger.

How could he possibly inflict that on Cassie or Elaine? Elaine had certainly been through enough with Caleb.

Then another thought crept into his mind, totally unwanted: he didn't have to be a field operative. No, he could work from a desk.

He brushed the idea away. It didn't suit him at all.

Even if thoughts of Elaine slipped into every corner of his mind, a tempting wraith.

Chapter Ten

The rising sun brought no answers about anything. Devlin showed off his cooking skills, such as they were, by making eggs, toast and bacon.

"You learned something," his mother said.

"Well, sometimes I *do* have to feed myself without a restaurant handy."

It pleased him to hear Elaine chuckle. Cassie managed her bacon easily. He'd made her egg over hard, so once Elaine cut it into manageable pieces, Cassie handled them well. He realized he might have been thinking the child was more disabled than she was.

Maybe he should start paying attention to what Cassie did for herself. Like giving Kittie, who was on her lap, tiny pieces of egg white. Kittie kept lifting her head; Devlin suspected the cat would prefer the bacon. Hardly surprising. He preferred it himself.

Elaine looked well rested and more relaxed this morning. Whatever had disturbed her about the calf mutilation and the alien-party invasion, she seemed to have let go for now.

"Are you working today?" he asked.

She shook her head. "Since I was out so late last night, Gage told me to relax today."

He had to grin. "So you might relax until what? Midday?"

She responded with a sly smile. "Are you reading me, Mr. Foreign Officer?"

"Learning you. I wish I was psychic." That would have avoided a whole lot of problems in life, and he wouldn't have needed to use assets like Niko.

Elaine looked at Cassie. "I'd like to be psychic, too."

He bet she would. The lack of communication must be one of the most frustrating parts of Cassie's condition. There had to be other frustrations, too. He'd noticed that the only time Cassie would allow her mother to touch her was bath and bedtime, and maybe dressing her. He certainly hadn't seen any hugs, and Elaine didn't strike him at all as a cold person.

"Is anything going to be done about that calf?" If anyone had discussed it, he hadn't heard. Hardly surprising, when he'd busied himself with other things.

"A necropsy. Mitch apparently isn't going to be satisfied with the idea of a predator. I don't think he really wants to have a necropsy, either."

"How come?"

"Because some of his neighbors are going to wonder if he's lost his marbles. Cattle mutilations don't happen around here, and the general attitude is that people are mistaking normal predation for something else."

He finished wiping egg from his plate with toast. "What do *you* think?"

She shook her head. "I have no real information. A dead calf. Looks weird, but maybe it's not. I'm going to trust Mitch's eventual estimation, though. He knows a whole lot more about cattle and predators than I ever will."

WHEN SALLY ARRIVED late in the morning to work with Cassie, Devlin and Elaine set out for Maude's to find something for dinner so Lu wouldn't have to cook.

"I should go grocery shopping for the clan, carry my weight," Devlin remarked.

"Your mom seems to enjoy doing it. Probably because it's a chance for her to change scenery and people." Elaine sighed. "I don't know how or why she keeps helping this way. Yeah, Cassie's her granddaughter, but nearly full-time childcare? Especially with a kid who's autistic? That's a whole lot."

"Well then, I'll give her money for groceries. Hell, she's the one who taught me to pay my way."

Elaine laughed but found herself wondering why he hadn't responded to what she had said about his mom dealing with an autistic granddaughter. The question nagged at her. Did he disapprove?

At Maude's, while standing at the counter waiting for takeout and a couple of lattes, Elaine scanned the room. Scanning rooms like this came with her job. She always took in the people around, looking for any kind of trouble.

But then she noticed two young women sitting in one of the booths. They had cheap plastic alien masks on the table between them and salads in front of them.

They stared at Devlin, then quickly looked away when they saw her looking at them. Something about that struck her as furtive. Were they just curious? But why? Those women were the strangers in town.

Or maybe… She was smiling as they walked out the door with food bags and the cups of hot coffee in their hands.

"I think you've got admirers," she told Devlin.

"Huh? Why?" He looked as if he didn't realize that was possible.

"Two young women in the café. They were eyeballing you. Then, when they knew I saw them, they looked away. They appeared embarrassed." She laughed. "If you were wondering if you still have it…"

But he responded oddly. "Yeah?" he said quietly, thoughtfully. "I'll catch up in a minute. I meant to get a slice of peach pie."

He turned around and strode back into Maude's.

And Elaine was too much of a cop to believe he was going back for pie. So two women admiring him was enough to get him to go back to check it out?

Not Devlin, not for a couple of women. He wasn't the type, as far as she could tell. Too mature for that kind of reaction, probably.

So what the hell was going on?

She kept walking, but slowly, waiting for him as she took some sips of her coffee. Maybe she could find out something when he rejoined her.

But that was another thing about Devlin she'd figured out. He kept a lot to himself. She was sure he wasn't even being totally forthcoming about his work.

Nope. She hated it. The cop in her hated it. She needed her answers.

DEVLIN WALKED BACK into Maude's and went up to the counter to get that peach pie, his cover story. Then he looked around the café as he waited and saw the two young women Elaine must have been referring to.

He caught them looking at him, then turn away as if embarrassed. He'd seen that reaction from women before during his career. Shyness, or culture?

Something about them… They reminded him of someone, although he couldn't say who. He just knew that he'd never set eyes on the two of them. He had a great memory for faces.

After paying for the pie, he walked out to catch up with Elaine.

Something troubled him about those women. But what? Why? God, he had become far too paranoid. On the job was one thing. In normal life, it had no place.

Maybe.

WHEN THEY GOT back to the house, Sally was working with Cassie. She was thrilled with Cassie's reaction to the kitten and the way she was taking care of it.

"This is good," she said with a smile. "Another step for Cassie. Her progress between this visit and the last is great, Elaine. It's great. If she's ready to accept the kitten into her personal space, she'll accept something else, probably not too far down the road."

Elaine started smiling.

At the door, Sally looked back. "She's begun to expand her world, and this was a big step in that direction."

Devlin saw Elaine gaze at Cassie, who sat on the living room rug with her kitten, and caught the sheen of tears in her eyes. The expression of hope.

Without giving any thought, or at least not enough thought, he reached out to lay his arm across Elaine's shoulders and give her a gentle squeeze.

She glanced at him and smiled.

And she didn't move away.

ELAINE WAS OVERJOYED. She'd thought she'd seen improvement in Cassie, but Sally had just confirmed it. The cat had been such a wonderful idea, and now she was wondering what next. What else might she do to encourage a reaction like this?

But she knew better than to press it. Baby steps, at least for now. Although Kittie was proving to be more than a baby step.

She was acutely aware of Devlin's arm around her shoulders. In the midst of her joy, she needed to share this moment, to savor the warmth of being held, however loosely. To feel a man wrapped around her, holding the joy in and offering more of it.

At last, she tore her gaze from Cassie and smiled at him. It was okay, right? Cassie's uncle and godfather, her brother-in-law. Family.

Except, for just a few seconds, she didn't think of him that way at all. She saw him as a man who could easily walk away with her heart. Dangerous.

Just then, Lu emerged from the back of the house, running her fingers through her hair and yawning. "Wow, did I fall asleep! With Sally here, I just kinda let go, I guess. How's Cassie?"

"Sally thinks she made a huge step with the kitten. We can talk about it when you have a chance to wake up."

Lu's laugh was self-deprecating as she passed them to go into the kitchen.

Cassie continued to sit on the floor, cat in her lap, watching the adults.

"Kittie," she said, pointing to the kitten in her lap.

Elaine's heart stopped; then she could hold back the tears no longer. "Yes, Cassie, I see Kittie. She's beautiful and loves you."

Then her daughter's gaze wandered down to the cat, and the moment broke.

Well, not entirely. Elaine turned into Devlin's embrace, his arms closing around her, welcoming her. God, it felt so good.

"I WANT TO go to the office," Elaine announced after an easy lunch of ham sandwiches. "I need to catch up about last night. Is that okay, Lu?"

"It's always okay. Now, scat. Cassie and I will play with the cat or color unicorns."

"I need to take a walk," Devlin said.

They both stepped outside, Elaine to get into her patrol vehicle and Devlin to start striding into town.

He was troubled by the sense of familiarity he'd detected about those two young women. Nagged at him too much to ignore. In his job, he rarely ignored it when something nagged him.

He needed to figure out what had caught his attention. Or just to see if he reacted the same way. If not, it had been some kind of mental mistake. Unfortunately, mistakes happened.

ELAINE FOUND THE office buzzing. Those who weren't out on patrol gabbed about last night. They also still gabbed about the crowd down the street. A crowd that didn't seem to be diminishing. A crowd that was starting to become a nuisance, filling the street, lining the roads just outside town with camping gear.

Had those people come prepared to camp? She suspected at Roswell they had hotels and motels to house the crowd. Could all these people have come here without checking the accommodations?

Well, of course they must have checked, or there wouldn't be so much camping gear. Regardless, they still seemed to be having a rollicking time. Sharing UFO stories, arguing finer points of the theories that seemed to have sprung up like weeds. All in fun. So far.

Dang, something was making her thoughts scatter. Red lights? An alien invasion? Devlin? She almost laughed at herself as she entered the office.

Connie Parish was seated at one of the desks, and when she saw Elaine, she waved her over. Kerri Canady sat nearby with her Snowy.

"We're just discussing the messes," Connie said. "Or should I just call it the alien invasion? All of it, including the dead calf."

Kerri spoke. "The street party is going to become a serious problem before much longer. People found it kind of fun and funny when it first started. They were even making money off it. But now?" She shrugged.

"Well," Elaine said dryly, "we don't live in a time when the sheriff could strap on his six-gun and throw people out of town."

Connie grinned. "I wish. I bet the city council is going to want to do something about it if this goes on much longer."

"Agreed," said Kerri.

"At least they're not causing trouble," Elaine remarked. "So far."

"Probably because they're smoking instead of drinking," Connie said.

Elaine joined her laughter.

Kerri spoke. "You could get high walking past them."

Elaine snorted. "No kidding."

Guy Redwing joined them. He'd taken to letting his hair grow longer, part of his Native American heritage. As a detective, he wore plain clothes. "We could start arresting them for the pot," he said. "That ought to make most of them head out of town. Or we could have a riot."

"Yeah," Kerri said. "There's that. I'll skip the riot."

Elaine grinned, enjoying herself. "Don't they outnumber us now?" Then her enjoyment slipped away. "Hey, you heard anything about Mitch Cantrell's calf?"

"I just heard," Guy answered. "He's firing two ranch hands. They were supposed to be keeping an eye on things last night and it seems they wandered away. Quite a way, given the calf."

Elaine shook her head. "Not good. But it still doesn't give us an answer unless those guys mutilated the calf themselves."

Humor vanished. All of them were troubled.

AROUND THE PARTIERS hung a cloud of marijuana smoke, an easily identifiable aroma. Devlin figured half the people here could get high without smoking anything. He smiled and looked around.

Some "aliens" draped themselves against lampposts. Long lines of them sat on the curbs. Others, heedless of traffic, stood in the streets, talking and laughing. Some even danced. Music played from several different locations. Yeah, a party.

A big, funny-looking party of green and silver and black. A lot of bug-eyed masks and one stand-out who had managed to make himself over into a praying mantis. How did mantises get into the alien world? He guessed his education was lacking. Though he had no intention of expanding it.

A surprising number of people actually talked about their reasons for being here, and it wasn't just for a party with like-minded others. They were quite serious about the Roswell crash, about Area 51, about the hangar at Wright-Patterson AFB that supposedly housed alien bodies. Or even live aliens. That, Devlin discovered, was quite an argument among these believers.

He found others recounting tales of crash retrievals, insisting there were many of them. Some said modern technology sprang from the crashed spaceships.

Then there was the abduction argument. Were they or weren't they? The cattle-mutilation discussion, which, surprisingly, varied between only two opinions: government or aliens. That was when he became certain that some of the conversations were being exaggerated by illicit substances.

A group of five was having a heated argument about whether these aliens came from the future, creatures that had evolved from humans a million years in the future or from a different planet. That group laid out plenty of reasons for their opinions, reasons that might have been fun for Devlin to listen to at a different time.

If he got that Vulcan peace sign one more time, though, he might growl.

But while he measured the crowd, his own passport of a green bug-eyed mask on the back of his head, he sought anything that might keep alerting him about being watched.

It was an odd sensation. It didn't feel like a hard focus but rather a blurry one, as if something hadn't yet clicked for the watcher.

But concern for Elaine, Cassie and his mother kept him moving among the people, stopping occasionally to throw a word or two into a conversation. He had to appear to belong with this group to avoid drawing the wrong kind of attention. Standard operating procedure.

The crowd could provide cover for anyone, himself included, and it would be hard to pick anyone out in this crazily dressed mob. He had to content himself with watching people's actions. Interpreting their meaning even though not always clear, but that was apparently his only tool here.

Still, the feeling of being watched wouldn't go away, whether strong or weak. And he was getting past the point of telling himself that his job had made him too paranoid.

The huge question looming in his mind, one that he'd been unable to resolve, was *who* in this place would be watching him and *why*.

He'd been away from this town for over fifteen years. Nobody held a grudge for that long, not that he could remember having left any grudges behind him.

So what and why? And only one answer came to him: his job in intelligence. Being a field officer running assets. He'd done that in more than one location in his career, but the risks were always the same. If the bad guys found out you were the officer running assets, your life became a target. *You* became a target.

Even so, why the hell would anyone have followed him here, of all places? And how would they have managed that since his own office had clamped a lid on his whereabouts.

He closed his eyes, gritted his teeth and faced it directly. Someone had leaked information about him. Maybe the same someone who had leaked Niko's identity.

A rats' nest that needed rooting out.

Then he heard a quiet voice that came from somewhere in the crowd, not too close, standing out only because of the accent.

His eyes popped open, and he looked around. He knew that accent.

Just as he had thought he recognized the two women at Maude's.

No reason that any person from that part of the world should be here.

And no reason they should not. This UFO crowd appeared to be pretty international in its membership.

But those few words in that accent stuck with him. A woman. Maybe. Replaying that snatch of conversation in his head, he realized he couldn't be *sure* if it had been a man or a woman. Too little of it. Voices varied in both genders, making it impossible to judge gender with surety.

Instead of going home to check on his family like he wanted, he kept circulating, listening for that accent, but he didn't hear it again.

Damn!

"I THOUGHT I told you to take the day off," Gage Dalton said to Elaine as he entered the office. "You've been working more hours than you realize."

"So has everyone else," Elaine answered, bridling a bit even though she truly liked Gage and didn't usually mind his fatherly concern.

"I've been giving people comp time as I can. This is yours. I don't even know why you came in today."

"To catch up on the scuttlebutt."

Gage laughed, the sound raspy. "I'll tell you when the necropsy reports come in. Or if Mitch figures it all out. You won't be out of the loop just because you're not here."

So she snatched up her light uniform jacket and headed out to her vehicle. The extra time with Cassie would certainly be welcome. Gage was right. She should never have gone in. She should have stayed home with her daughter.

So what had gotten into her? Sharing a house with a man who had begun to make her nerves tingle with a yearning she didn't want?

Yeah, probably. But he was going to be here awhile, from what he'd said and was entitled to visit his mother. End of subject.

Her guilt was ebbing, though. Slowly settling into her heart like a warm touch, she felt Caleb close to her. Felt that Caleb would want her to get on with her life and wouldn't mind if she had a thing with his brother.

Caleb had been rough around the edges, the result, no doubt, of the construction work he did and the people he was around all the time. But he'd never lost a heart as big as the whole outdoors.

No, he would want her to be happy in whatever package that happiness came.

She'd known that all along, of course, but she hadn't *felt* it. Now she was beginning to.

Still, a sexual relationship with a guy who'd be leaving soon and most likely permanently, given his past?

No way. She wasn't the type for flings and didn't want any more heartache. Nor did she want to expose Cassie to any fleeting relationships.

Having settled that in her mind, she came home to a potential crisis. Cassie was sitting on the living room floor, cat in her arms, looking mulish. Lu sat on the couch, perplexed. Elaine's mother radar immediately started pinging.

"What's wrong, Lu?"

Lu sighed. "I don't think it's major, but when I wanted Cassie to come for a walk with me or even sit on the porch, she wouldn't because she doesn't want to be separated from the kitten."

"Oh, man." Elaine dropped onto one of the recliners and regarded her daughter. There was nothing in the world as immovable as Cassie when she got stubborn. So what now? She knew what that kitten would do if allowed outside. It would go exploring, and judging by her bouts of hyperactivity indoors, Kittie would get distracted by something and be off like a shot.

Just as she was thinking that, Kittie stood, stretched, then dashed off Cassie's lap, running around the living room, climbing the back of the couch and just otherwise being exuberant.

"I see a cat tree coming," Elaine remarked.

Lu nodded. "Might be a good idea. I'll remind Devlin he said he'd get one."

Cassie was watching her cat's antics with obvious delight. Okay, then.

Rising, Elaine said, "I'm going to change, Lu. Then I'll rummage through the things that Mike Windwalker sent home with us. Maybe I'll find something there. I know he sent toys I need to get out."

"Good idea," Lu said.

"And if I don't find a solution there, I'll call Mike. We can't let Cassie become a recluse because of Kittie."

MIKE HAD INDEED sent them home with a great deal more than a litter box and litter. Elaine felt silly for not having looked through the bag earlier, but it had become an ingrained habit not to introduce too much to Cassie at once. The cat had seemed enough for a beginning. And what a beginning!

Opening the bag at last, she found a collection of toys.

Some were balls, soft and fuzzy or with shiny fringe, toys that bounced on strings at the end of wands. One of them looked like a praying mantis, of all things.

But at the very bottom, she found something that looked like a harness. Pulling it out, she studied it, figuring out how to use it and wondering if it might be too soon for some of this, even though the kitten needed play.

God, did most parents have to make these kinds of decisions all the time? Maybe. On the spectrum or not, kids depended on parents to take care of them.

The harness, she decided. Cassie needed to be able to go outside, and for now she refused to be separated from Kittie.

How much would the cat struggle against this? Elaine snorted. What were a few scratches?

She checked once again to make sure she understood how it should fit, to minimize disturbance or fear for the cat. To limit it for Cassie's benefit as well.

Out in the living room, Cassie was still watching Kittie play rock climber on the curtains, climbing up and down as fast as her little paws would carry her. Cassie, wonder of wonders, was grinning.

Elaine sat cross-legged across from her daughter and held up the bright pink harness. Cassie dragged her gaze from the cat to the harness and then to her mother's face. Her expression had begun to darken.

Lu called from the kitchen. "I was bad and made us cinnamon rolls. You want some coffee?"

"Love some in a few minutes."

Cassie still regarded that harness with suspicion.

"Honey," Elaine said quietly, "this is for kittens. It's like a dog's leash. It won't hurt her."

Cassie tightened her lips. Elaine tensed inside. Was this about to go seriously bad?

"Just think. If she wears this, she can go outside with you. Sit on the porch. Go for walks with Grandma Lu. Maybe even chase butterflies in the park. But she won't get lost. She'll always stay with you."

Elaine sat quietly, waiting, wondering how much had truly gotten through or if Cassie had stopped listening before the explanation was complete.

Cassie had a bulldog determination about some things, but others, if they lost her interest, couldn't get past some kind of internal resistance.

Finally, however, Cassie's face smoothed over. Not by any means did she offer agreement, but the resistance was clearly gone.

Rising, Elaine went to pry Kittie from the curtains. As soon as she was cradled in Elaine's arm, the cat grew still and began to purr. A good temperament.

Then, sitting facing Cassie again, Elaine slipped her forearm forward between the cat's four paws and beneath her chin.

It turned out to be easier than she had anticipated to slip the harness over Kittie's head, down around her chest and midsection, then gently tighten it until it fit. Just like that.

Someone with experience had created that design.

Then Kittie leaped easily into Cassie's lap and began to purr up a storm.

"Kittie," her daughter said, and began to pet her new best friend.

Elaine's throat tightened, and she had to hold back tears. Such a good thing for Cassie. A friend. A companion she didn't fear. Warm and cuddly, the only kind of cuddle Cassie had so far accepted.

That cat was a miracle.

Elaine rose from the floor and went to the kitchen to join Lu. For the first time, she realized how tense she had been because her knees started to feel a bit shaky. So afraid, she guessed, that something might have gone badly wrong. The only thing in the world that could make her this fearful anymore was Cassie. Every single step was fraught with danger for Cassie. Never, ever did she want to set her daughter back.

It might be the biggest fear of her life.

"I watched," Lu said quietly. "That was brilliant."

"It was also scary."

Lou poured coffee into the mug in front of Elaine. "I was holding *my* breath. You were good, though. Calm and gentle but kinda firm, too. I think Cassie's responding better, Elaine."

Elaine nodded, cupping her mug in both hands. "I hope so. The cat has been a boon, for sure."

Lu laughed quietly. "I never thought I'd have been so glad to see an animal on my kitchen table."

That drew a laugh from Elaine, too. "Listen, I'm going to try putting the leash on Kittie and see if I can get them onto the porch. Gently."

No pushing it. Quiet, careful suggestions.

Sitting on the floor once again in front of her daughter, who watched the hijinks of a kitten who wanted to explore and climb everything in the room, Elaine made her suggestion.

Keeping her voice quiet and cheerful, she said, "Do you want to take Kittie onto the porch? She might like a little sunshine. I know *you* would. What do you think?"

Cassie gazed at her from a smooth face. Okay, no objection, then.

Rising, she went to get Cassie's jacket and the leash, then pulled on her own jacket.

"Lu? Cassie's going to take her kitten outside."

"Lord," she heard Lu say from the kitchen. One word that conveyed hope and trepidation.

Elaine knelt, speaking to Cassie to explain what she was doing. "See? This is how the leash clips into the harness. None of this will hurt Kittie, but it means she can come everywhere with you now."

Cassie seemed to like that idea. She stood up, but when Elaine offered her the end of the leash, she didn't take it.

Okay, small steps. Or huge ones, now that she'd gotten the kitten harnessed and her daughter willing to make a trip out front with it. All this was a wonderful leap that had been very much needed. Maybe more leaps were around the corner.

So she opened the front door and led Kittie by the leash onto the porch. The kitten balked a little at first, but it didn't take her long to figure out that if she went forward a whole new world of scents and sounds existed. Curiosity had won the day.

Outside the late afternoon had begun to blow a slightly chilly breeze off the mountains, but it hadn't become cold. Elaine gave Kittie her head, letting her roam the whole porch while Cassie sat on her little chair, watching. Then Kittie jumped up on the porch rail, and Cassie shrieked a delighted laugh.

Elaine's heart nearly stopped. She wanted to hear that sound from her solemn daughter again and again.

Then Cassie reached a hand out to Elaine. Understanding, her heart beating happily, she turned the end of the leash over to her daughter. "Just make sure not to let it drop. Kittie will run off to explore everything, and that's not safe for her, okay?"

Cassie responded in no way other than tightening her hand around the pink loop of the leash.

Elaine sat on one of the lawn chairs and watched every single second. One cat. One little girl stepping a tiny bit out of her shell. Was there anything more beautiful?

She could have stayed there the rest of the day watching, but after about fifteen minutes, Kittie landed back in Cassie's lap. Cassie stood, cradling her furry friend, and turned toward the door.

Time to go inside.

Inside, Elaine took the leash off Kittie but left the harness on so the kitten could get used to it.

Elaine released a long breath, letting go of the tension that had been stretching every nerve. She'd passed through hidden dangers without once upsetting Cassie.

DEVLIN DIDN'T RETURN to the house immediately. He was troubled by the accent he'd heard. Troubled by the increasing feeling that someone in his group might have betrayed him, a sensation that made his skin crawl. Everyone in field operations depended on secrecy for their lives. What if someone had failed him?

Not that anyone should. But then, the whole world had heard about the name of a female operative who had been publicly exposed for no better reason than vengeance. That's all it took to violate national security and throw agents and assets to the wolves. One man's need for power and his hatred of being proved wrong. Other than that, the woman's exposure had benefited not a single soul but may have cost lives.

What made him certain he wasn't in the same boat?

The fact that they'd yanked him home so swiftly after Niko's cover had been blown? That he'd been instantly protected?

But only one person was needed who liked to flaunt his or her knowledge just to display importance.

Devlin didn't often lose his cool. His career had long since taught him that was the most dangerous thing he could do. But he wanted to lose his cool just then.

Had he been deluding himself? Had he believed he was protected by his colleagues more than he was? Had he exposed his entire family to danger? Had he, God forbid, trusted too much?

The idea made him want to smash something. Then he felt sickened. If you couldn't trust your own people charged with your protection, the ones who worked closely with you and knew most of your secrets, who *could* you trust?

Nobody. Maybe he ought to just pack up and get out of here. If someone was following him, they could follow him to somewhere else, away from the people he cared about.

The more he thought about it, the less he wanted to go back to the house, exposing his mother, his sister-in-law, his niece to whatever might be chasing him. Uncaring that he might be exposing his back, he strode out of town, then a short way down the state highway, hearing and feeling the blast of air as the big trucks raced past him in the dimming late-afternoon light.

A huge problem gnawed at him, though. If someone had followed him here—and the tingling sensation at the base of his skull argued that they had—then his leaving might not help at all.

He cursed in several languages and walked faster. He hated that he might have been playing the fool all along.

Confident in his colleagues and allies at the agency. God, a damn clerk could have become a serious problem.

Realizing he was far enough out of town now to have a conversation that couldn't be heard, he pulled his satellite phone from his pocket, pressed the button to encode his conversation and then dialed a memorized number.

As he listened to the connection click through, he turned and saw those two baleful red lights. Wondered again what they could be, made a silent promise to himself to check them out soon, ignoring the fact that he should be long gone before he had the chance.

"Hi, John."

"Hey, Dev," said a familiar voice at the other end. "I thought you were taking a vacation. What's up?"

"Am I being followed?"

Silence greeted him. Then: "Why the hell would you think that?"

"A feeling. An accent I heard. If I am, just say so and I'll get the hell out of here now."

"How about I don't know where *here* is?" John fell silent. Then: "Seriously, Dev?"

"Unless I've gone off the deep end and started to imagine things, yeah. I'm being watched."

John cussed vociferously. "A feeling? Hell, man, I know that feeling. Maybe you should just get the hell out of wherever you are now."

Devlin hesitated, then took the dangerous step of revelation, trusting John because they'd been friends throughout his entire career. Because he had to trust *someone*. "Biggest mistake I made was coming home to visit. I clear out, fine, but what if someone thinks my family knows where the hell I've gone?"

A long silence from John. Devlin could imagine his

surprise at learning that Devlin had a family. Another closely guarded secret, although easy to keep when he never came home.

Then John offered, "We're still looking for the leak that betrayed your asset. That info had to have come from here. We'll find whoever it is."

"Small help now. Whoever betrayed him might well know where I am to judge by the way I'm feeling now."

"Your location is being protected. Hardly anyone should know where you are."

"Who should have known about Niko? You know they had to identify him through me. That's why I was pulled out. Come on, John." But now a new kind of tension was creeping along his spine. This conversation was beginning to make him wonder if he could trust John.

John paused again. "I'll speed up the search for the traitor on our end. Clearly this can't drag out. But you get the hell out of there if you can. As soon as you can."

"John." Not a question but a warning.

"Yeah?"

"Be careful. Someone can't be trusted." And if it was John, the man's tracks would be buried so deep they might never find him. And now John knew too much. Or maybe he'd known too much all along. He'd said he didn't know where Devlin was, but that might be bull. Devlin cussed again, silently.

John answered, "Hell, man. You think I'm too dense to figure that out?"

After completing the call, Devlin shoved the sat phone into his jacket pocket and turned, heading home. Now he had a bushel of new worries. But no, it couldn't have been John. John had no irons in the fire when it came to Eastern Europe.

But secretaries and others were damn-near invisible and almost always around. Just one example of people who could learn things they weren't supposed to know. Locals who had security clearances, which made too many people lax with secrets.

He thought about Cassie, that sweet child, and Elaine and his mother. About three people he needed to protect somehow. About how he might have brought a threat to their door.

God, he hated himself. And hated himself even more because deep inside, he knew part of the reason he didn't want to leave: he had come to crave Elaine with a deep, piercing ache. A need so strong it could have brought him to his knees.

ONCE DEVLIN RETURNED, Lu heated up dinner. It was kind of late for Cassie, but Elaine didn't want to complain about that, especially since Cassie seemed quite content with Kittie.

It was usually bad to disrupt the schedule, but this time Cassie didn't appear at all disturbed by the change. Another bit of progress? Or was it just temporary because Cassie was distracted?

Elaine sighed quietly, accepting that she would never know until someday when Cassie chose to talk. If she ever did.

It felt good to have Devlin home, though. He stayed in the kitchen, helping his mother as much as he could, a solid and somehow reassuring presence.

Even so, Elaine felt a subdued tension in him, and she didn't like it. Had something bad happened? Damn, she was beginning to think that Devlin shared about as much as Cassie did.

So different from his brother. Caleb had always seemed so open, so ready to talk about things in his life or in Elaine's life. Considering how far away Caleb often worked, video calls hadn't been enough. Certainly hadn't been intimate enough. But once he came home, intimacy thrived in every sense.

And yes, very different from Devlin, who sometimes struck her as a locked box of secrets.

After dinner, a bit restless, she stepped outside onto the porch, wrapping a sweater around herself to withstand the spring chill in the air. In another hour or so, it would be too cold out here without a winter jacket. A single spring day sometimes ran through all four seasons.

The breeze, stirred by the changing temperature between land and mountains, was gentle. Later it would grow stronger, icier, but right now it was a soft caress with chilly fingers.

Before long, however, she felt something besides the breeze's touch. She felt something far more, something that made her feel downright creepy. Part of her was afraid to look, a ridiculous reaction for someone who lived life in law enforcement with each day bringing the possibility of true danger.

Annoyed with herself, she turned slowly, trying to penetrate the nocturnal spaces, the dark holes amid tree branches, the shadowy places created by the deepening night.

Of course she saw nothing, no matter how often she peered into the night. Vision was odd in the darkness, though. Things seemed to move even when they didn't. The brain tried to turn amorphous shapes into something familiar.

It was a waste of time to stand here like this.

Just as she was about to give in to this uncharacteristic feeling and go indoors, Devlin joined her. The springs on the storm door creaked.

At first, he didn't say anything as he came to stand beside her. Then, a minute or so later, he asked, "Are you okay?"

"Why wouldn't I be?" she answered, reluctant to reveal the crazy sensation of being watched. Even though she'd learned it was rarely imagination. But who the hell would be watching?

"I dunno. It's just that since I got here, you've never come out to stand alone here in the dark."

"And that's such a long time," she answered, a trifle tartly, forcing herself to shed the uneasy feeling.

He chuckled quietly.

Then, astonishing her, he drew her into a snug embrace. Elaine wanted to melt. Wanted to give in to the softening he caused inside her. Never wanted to move away.

KALINA AND ZOE watched from the bushes, looking through the night at the porch, where their target stood with a woman.

Zoe sighed. "He never goes anywhere we can use the poison."

"Never. It's going to have to be messy." The gun. She wasn't afraid of it. She'd had to kill before. But this was different. One man, not a mob or part of a so-called army. They had always fought to protect others.

But even the need for vengeance didn't make this feel right. Anger had subsided. Now Kalina had begun to wonder why they'd been sent to kill one man. Did they think he knew too much? That he still had contacts like Niko?

She and her sister had been led here, pushed here, driven here. All to kill one man.

She had begun to view the mission in a very different way. Very. "Zoe? Has this mission begun to feel wrong somehow?"

Zoe didn't answer immediately. When she did, her answer remained firm. "Maybe we don't know everything. But we know what we need to do. For Niko. Maybe for something bigger."

"I don't think we were sent for Niko. A life for a life?" That kind of measurement had always struck her as distasteful.

Again, Zoe fell silent for a minute or two. "Maybe not."

But they knew they'd been ordered to complete this task. Failure to do so would cost them everything. As it had cost Niko.

Kalina stuck her hand in her pocket and felt the pistol. Was it time to load it?

Then Zoe surprised her. "We have to take care not to kill the two women and the child."

"I know." That kind of killing was the reason they had fought at home. To end it.

But how could they possibly succeed?

Chapter Eleven

In the living room, after Lu had gone to bed, Elaine and Devlin sat quietly in the two recliners, an end table between them. One table lamp cast a golden glow. The heat kicked on, first blowing cold, then warm air into the room.

Peaceful. Except it wasn't peaceful to Elaine because she sensed that Devlin was tightly coiled. What was he tense about? Damn it, she was getting tired of wondering and never learning much about him. He was here in the house with her daughter. Her initial instinct was that he was part of the family, that she could probably trust him. But shouldn't she know more? Especially when he seemed unable to relax himself?

Almost as if reading her mind, Devlin spoke. "I'm going to tell you about my situation. Then I'd like you to tell me whether you think it's better for me to remain or go."

"Why is there a decision?" Now tension creeped along her own nerve endings. A *decision*?

"Each has its advantages, but let me tell you a bit about myself and why I'm here."

"So it's not just for your mom." Elaine snorted. "I didn't think so. After all these years? Right. So dump. I want to know everything." Not that she believed she'd get everything from him. Box of secrets.

"I know I said I work for the State Department. I actually work for the CIA. As a field operative."

"What's that?" Then Elaine shook her head. "That State Department claim must be wearing thin after all this time."

"Not really. I doubt you have any idea how many people work at most embassies or consulates."

She sighed, wishing he'd come to the point. "Probably not."

"It's a lot of people. Everyone knows there are intelligence operations everywhere, including foreign agencies, but pointing out the officers is hard in the crowd."

"Okay." She waited, holding on to her patience, which was growing thinner as he moved through all these details.

"Long story short," he said, "as a field operative, I worked overseas out of embassies over the years. It was my job to recruit assets. Local people who could provide important intelligence. One of my assets was exposed and killed. I was yanked out immediately for fear that the asset had been exposed because *my* cover was blown, and they didn't want more of my assets to be exposed. Hell, that was the last thing *I* wanted. I had to get lost until they could find the leak."

"So you thought you could get lost by coming *home*?" Anger began to replace her tension. "Devlin… Oh, man." She couldn't even finish.

"I thought no one would think of my hometown because I'd hardly visited in so many years."

"Not since Cassie's baptism," she snapped. "Which wasn't that long ago."

"I never revealed I was coming here. Habit after all these years."

"Oh, God, Devlin." Elaine jumped up from her chair and started pacing. "What you're telling me is somebody knows you're here and it might be dangerous. How could you?"

She turned, putting her hands on her hips and glaring. "How am I supposed to protect Cassie from whatever you've dragged to my doorstep?"

"That's what I want to talk to you about."

"A bit late, isn't it? Let me wrap my mind around this before we discuss protecting Cassie and your mom. God, Devlin," she repeated and resumed pacing. Fury had overtaken her, and she needed to get a grip before it screwed up her ability to think. She'd controlled anger many times in her job, but not rage like this. A whole new level. So much anger that she couldn't even face the anguish of betrayal buried somewhere in this mess.

Two circuits around the room and she spoke again. "Somebody had to know you were here."

"Nobody should."

She paced some more, then faced him again, jabbing her finger at him. "So you're being protected by a sieve?"

She heard his voice grow tight with anger. "So it would seem."

"God, I can't believe this. I'm not going to drive you out of here right this instant only because I believe that *you* believed no one would find you."

She dropped onto the edge of the recliner seat. "Damn it, Devlin, what about Cassie?"

THAT WAS THE QUESTION, Devlin thought as he watched Elaine react, felt her reaction to his very core. Fury fulminated in him, fueled by betrayal, fear for his family and a need to take this assassin out of the picture permanently.

How could anyone have found him here in this out-of-the-way two-stoplight town?

He had records at the company, of course. Impossible not to. But the only place this town should have been mentioned was when he applied for this job and his security clearance. And once he was vetted, that info was classified and locked away.

"I've been trying to figure out how anyone could have found me here. Anything mentioning this place ought to be buried almost as deep as nuclear secrets. As for me being linked to my asset? That's truly a big worry."

She looked at him, still angry, but a hint of sorrow was forming in her expression. She'd lost trust in him. He couldn't blame her.

"Leaving isn't good," she said. "If they lose track of you, they might come looking for information from us." Then she shook her head. "And if you stay…" She didn't complete the thought.

His heart squeezed from the pain he'd brought her. "I've been having the same thoughts. That's why I wanted to talk to you about the choices. I don't give a damn about myself. The family here, that's all that matters. You're the one with skin in this game. I can be gone by morning."

She sat for a long time, thinking. So long that he started to wonder if she was thinking about more than this situation.

When at last she got around to speaking, she astonished him. "We've got to get rid of this assassin, Devlin. You can't have him chasing you all over the place and I refuse to have to worry indefinitely about Cassie and Lu. So we need to make a plan. Capture or kill. And I'm not apologizing for threatening to kill. Not under these circumstances."

He'd brought her to that. He hated himself. *Loathed* himself.

She stood. "Let's make coffee and start talking about how to deal with this mess."

No, he hadn't expected her to take on this problem. He'd thought she'd want him to leave as quickly as possible to draw the threat away from Cassie and Lu.

But she was a law enforcement officer. Of course. She wasn't designed to run from anything.

KALINA AND ZOE spent a cold night in dark spaces created by trees and shrubbery not far down the street from the house where the man stayed. They tried to take turns sleeping, but the chill prevented it.

It had to be something more than the weather, Zoe thought. At home, they'd spent more than one freezing night in the mountains and had managed to gather some sleep.

So it was nerves, she decided. She and Kalina were experiencing the kind of fear they'd felt when they faced a battle. One man was not a battle. Except that this had become a battle, an internal one.

This man, too, was a soldier, an enemy soldier. But his family wasn't.

She understood the turmoil that afflicted Kalina. Life hadn't prepared them for this kind of mission.

Assassin. The word floated into her mind for the first time and remained, leaving a sour taste in her mouth. Leaving her stomach twisting with nausea.

Who had sent them and why?

She turned to look at her sister and saw the same question reflected in Kalina's face. *Were they being used?*

BEFORE DAWN, Elaine's phone rang. The department. She listened, murmuring some answers, then hung up. She looked at Devlin.

"And thus, the mystery of mutilated calf is solved. It apparently died from a sudden pneumonia and a couple of dogs had apparently chewed on it. Two of Mitch Cantrell's range hands found the carcass, drained it, cut it up some, then delivered it to the spot near the UFO hunters. They thought it was funny."

All Devlin could do was shake his head.

"Yeah," Elaine said. "They've been fired. Anyway, it's time to wake everyone up."

LU WANTED ANSWERS before she would pack up Cassie and head for her sister's house in Glenwood Springs. Devlin decided to leave the answers to Elaine, primarily because Cassie was involved. It went without saying that Elaine was a better judge of how Cassie might perceive this sudden move.

Although, how that could be smoothed over, Devlin had no idea.

"It's a special trip." A simple explanation, offered in a steely tone to Lu, shorter than Devlin would have offered. But then, he'd become pretty good over the years at spinning a longer yarn.

Lu looked worriedly at him but he kept his lips zipped. Elaine's tone and his silence apparently told Lu quite enough. Her lips tightened, her eyes darkened. When she spoke her voice, much like Elaine's, was threaded with steel.

"I don't know what's going on, and I'm sure I probably don't want to know. We'll pack up right now, and I'll call Suze on the road."

She turned sharply on her heel and marched toward the hallway. "And, damn it, make breakfast for Cassie. Now. At least some cereal."

"And a thermos of coffee for Lu," Devlin added quietly. He headed straight for the pot.

Outside, dawn had just started to break, washing the world in that odd blue color that came before the reddish-orange brilliance of the rising sun, flattening the light until shadows could hardly be seen. Concealing more than Devlin would like.

But Elaine managed to impress him yet again. She encouraged a sleepy Cassie to eat while telling her that she and Grandma were going to Aunt Suze's house for a visit. The child visibly brightened, but said only one word: "Kittie."

"Yes, Kittie will go with you."

Lu snorted. "Yeah, a litter box in the car. Suze is going to love me."

Because of the cat, the trip involved more than strapping in a young child and a tote full of clothes. There was a carrying box. The litter box. The box of canned cat food. A bucket of cat litter. Cat toys.

Cassie only took her coloring book and crayons for herself.

"This *could* be amusing," Devlin remarked as he helped load the trunk of his mother's car with all the cat supplies.

Elaine just looked at it and shook her head. "We need a whole troop movement now. No cat sitter for that girl."

"Doesn't look like it," he agreed.

Casual conversation when he was sure neither of them

felt in the least casual. His neck was creeping again. A glance at Elaine suggested she detected it, too.

At last, they sent Lu, Cassie and Kittie on their way. The sun had risen above the eastern mountains, casting a golden glow over land that hadn't quite reached the fullness of spring yet.

The sight carried Devlin back to a place he didn't want to see ever again. Not since Niko had died. Not since he had been forced to face just how much of a danger he could be to those who helped him. Sure, the possibility was always there, but usually those assets were never revealed unless they did something to reveal themselves. Niko had done nothing. Of that his colleagues had been sure, hence yanking Devlin back to the United States.

No, the leak had come from within the protected walls of the intelligence service. A place where even a small leak could be deadly. And the people he had to rely on to locate it…well, one of them might be the leak.

Hellacious situation. He looked at Elaine as she watched the car carry her daughter away.

"This is going to be hard on Cassie," she remarked, her voice level. "Suze always comes *here* to visit."

"So this is really going to throw her out of her comfort zone?"

"Badly." She faced him then, anger glimmering in her eyes. "I'm going to get ready for work."

Part of the plan. Her putting on her uniform and making it look as if she went to work, and Devlin was alone. Except Elaine would be out there, watching.

However many days and nights it took.

Just one big lousy assumption on his part, and he'd come here to wreck everyone's life.

But he hadn't been alone in that assumption. Everyone

had assumed the leak had come from within the consulate itself, probably from one of the local employees who had tipped somehow to the information. No one had initially suspected that it could have come from higher up the food chain.

Nobody except the traitor, anyway. And if he or she was hunting for the leak, intent on concealing it, they could be in even deeper trouble. They'd have someone who didn't observe the guardrails, who couldn't be found. Yeah, they'd be in some deep dung.

So could all his assets and the assets of other field operatives.

He watched Lu's car turn the corner to head toward the state highway. At least those two were out of it.

He heard Elaine go into the house. She was now up to her neck in his problem.

Remove the assassin even if she had to kill him? That she had announced her willingness to do that sent a deep chill down his spine. God forbid he turn her into a killer.

ZOE AND KALINA saw the older woman and the very young child leave the house, drive away. Judging by the amount of things they had stacked in the trunk, it was going to be a long trip.

This gave the sisters a large dose of relief. Then the deputy had left the house in her official car and wearing her uniform.

Their target was alone. A clean kill.

But neither of them moved immediately. Throughout the night, questions had begun to seethe in them.

"Why couldn't they give us his name?" Zoe asked.

"So we couldn't tell it if we got caught before we killed him?" Kalina suggested.

They pondered that for a while. Then Kalina spoke again. "Why would they worry about that? We're not doing anything except traveling. We even have passports. Nobody will stop us."

"Until we kill him. Then everyone will know who our target was. It won't need to be secret anymore."

"But we're going to get away."

Zoe stared another question in the eye. "So why didn't they give us instructions like when we got here? Why don't they tell us where to go after this?"

Kalina offered no answer, but there didn't appear to be one. Fired up by the idea of avenging Niko, they hadn't asked enough questions, or so it now seemed. Not that they had been given an opportunity to question their mission.

The questions held them still as the morning brightened. They'd have to move before the cop came back from duty, but they still had time.

Time to wonder exactly what they'd been sent to do.

ELAINE CLIMBED AN evergreen tree in front of one of the older houses on the street. The height of her position gave her a nearly uninterrupted view of her house through binoculars.

She saw Devlin settle on the porch with a cup of coffee and wondered how he could possibly think that made him a target, out there in public in the bright light of day.

Any assassin would be wary of that setup. But then, coffee finished, he went inside the house, where contradictorily he made himself a better target. Concealed from any watchers who happened along the street.

But then there were the close quarters of the house. God, Elaine wished for a clearer picture of what might happen. How could she possibly know that the assassin wouldn't look like one of the town's residents, strolling along the sidewalk? Slipping into the house from the back.

Or maybe the guy wouldn't care, he'd take his shot while Devlin was outside then flee before anyone could react. A silencer. Yeah, it might conceal the sound of the gunshot enough that she could come home tonight and find Devlin dead.

Thoughts swirled in her mind, not making perfect sense as they turned one way and then another. Focus. She had to focus.

Then, making her heart nearly stop, she saw Devlin emerge from the house and start walking toward the edge of town. Where he'd be fully exposed. He was nuts.

Or very smart. Because then she saw two figures trying to move surreptitiously around bushes, right behind him. He was drawing them out.

She scrambled down from the tree as fast as she could, stripping her gloves when she reached the bottom because they were sticky with sap.

Unsnapping her holster. Getting ready.

Two of them? God, somebody definitely wanted to get rid of Devlin.

Then she began her own surreptitious tracking of those two figures. What if Devlin had no idea they were behind him?

DEVLIN WAS SURE the assassin was following him. That was the whole point of this little stroll of his. He'd often felt the guy watching him and had no reason to think he'd taken his eyes off his target.

No, he'd come. The only question was how Devlin

proposed to handle it. The guy probably meant to shoot him. So Devlin's entire life might depend on hearing the sound of a gun cock, not the noisiest sound in the world. As if the world wasn't full of many other sounds as the morning grew busier.

There was Elaine, of course. She'd gone to watch for exactly this. If she moved in time, they might be able to round the guy up before he took his shot.

But Devlin was really past caring. If he died, oh well. The important thing was to remove this threat from his family. His death would be a small price.

Although he would have liked to know who had betrayed him.

He kept marching along, moving at a casual speed as if suspecting nothing at all.

"Someone's following us," Zoe said. War had taught them to be hyperalert when necessary.

"Yes. I think it must be that woman cop."

"So today we die." They weren't afraid of that, either. They'd looked death in the face too many times. They just needed to know that they'd died for something important.

And right now, feeling that Niko's death might have been used to manipulate them, they weren't all that certain what they might be dying for.

They weren't far away from their target now. Zoe pulled out the gun.

Then Kalina said, "I can't."

Just as a woman on the right said, "Drop that gun now."

Turning their heads, they looked straight into the barrel of that cop's gun.

Without hesitation, Zoe dropped her pistol. They'd failed. The worst of it was that she didn't feel like a failure.

Then the two women dropped to their knees. Kalina started crying.

As their target approached them, Zoe looked at him and said, "I'm sorry." Then she closed her eyes, expecting to die.

IT ALL RESEMBLED a strange dream to Elaine. Weird. Hard to make sense of. Two women, one pointing a pistol at Devlin, then giving up instantly and dropping to their knees. One saying she was sorry and crying. The other simply looking resigned with her eyes closed.

My God, they thought they were going to die!

Galvanized, Elaine hurried over to them and kicked the pistol away. She knew she needed to cuff them, but a strong part of her rebelled for some reason. They had been about to murder a man. She shouldn't even hesitate.

Devlin came to stand about six feet in front of them. "You look familiar," he said quietly.

The woman who wasn't crying opened her eyes and said, "Niko."

Devlin swore, but it was a quiet sound. Full of sorrow.

Then he looked at Elaine. "Do you have to take them right in?"

Her heart was warring with the cop. Her heart won. "We can get coffee and some breakfast first."

It somehow felt like the right thing to do. She patted them down anyway.

THE HOUSE WAS eerily quiet without Lu, Cassie and Kittie. No movement. No little sounds. No greeting from the kitchen from Lu. Empty.

Elaine definitely didn't like the emptiness. Except it wasn't really. Not with Devlin and the two women here.

Order of priorities, maybe? Or just emotional attachments?

Didn't matter. Still armed, she went to make coffee.

Devlin and the two women sat at the kitchen table, he on the side facing them. While brewing the drip pot, she heard the first word. It came from Devlin.

"Niko," he said. Just one word.

She turned, folding her arms, listening. Those women shivered and looked hopeless. She almost felt sorry for them, except they had tried to kill Devlin.

One of them spoke, her words heavily accented. The one who had dropped the gun. "Niko was our brother."

A silence as heavy as lead settled in the room. Devlin didn't move a muscle. Both women looked at him with a glimmer of hatred but far more despair.

Finally, he said, "Kalina and Zoe."

The women looked startled, their gazes leaping first to him, then to each other.

"I am Zoe," said the one who'd held the gun. "How do you know?"

"Because Niko talked about you a few times. I know he was proud of you."

The other woman, who must be Kalina, looked down. "He betrayed us. You betrayed *him*."

Devlin drummed his fingers on the table, his face as dark as a midsummer storm. "Niko didn't betray you. Never once. He was working to help make you safe."

"But he…"

Devlin cut right through the protest. "Not everyone you trust is trustworthy. Do you understand me? There are some people you think are working with you who are working against you. Niko was hunting them. Yes, for me as well as you. So we could find out how bad it was, maybe find a way to stop it. But he never, *never* betrayed you."

Kalina drew a deep, shaky breath. "You betrayed Niko."

"Somebody betrayed *me*. That's how Niko was found."

Both women's heads snapped up. Then they faced each other, their expressions growing angry.

Zoe spoke. "We have been used." Then she looked at Devlin. "Do you know much about them?"

"Some. I was working on getting closer to uncovering them."

Kalina nodded. "They fear you. They feared Niko. And they must be the ones who sent us."

Zoe, frowning until the corners of her mouth nearly reached her chin, nodded as well. "We began to fear…" Then she shook her head. "Niko. They used Niko against us. To get you."

Then they put their heads on the table, buried on their arms. Quiet tears could be heard.

Elaine had made the coffee strong and poured cups full for everyone, and her overriding sense was sympathy for these women. She couldn't begin to imagine their heartbreak, having already been surrounded by so much loss and betrayal.

And she had no idea how she was going to put these two in a cell. There had to be some other way. As far as she could tell they'd been through enough hell and weren't likely to go around attempting to murder anyone else.

A few minutes passed; then Zoe and Kalina sat up, wiping their faces on their sleeves. Their expressions had turned solemn.

"We are soldiers," Kalina said. "You will punish us for what we have done. It will be just."

Just? Elaine was having a problem with that. She looked

at Devlin. "You're the diplomat. Find me a way around arresting them for attempted murder. If you want to."

A slow smile appeared on his face. "How about we just report them as illegals so they can go home? If that's what they want." Then he looked at them. "How did you get into this country?"

"Consul in San Francisco."

Devlin shook his head. "Well, they can't go there. Don't know how much of a vipers' nest that might be. In fact, this whole situation may have put Kalina and Zoe in a great deal of danger from more than one direction."

He leaned back, clearly thinking. "I need to call someone."

Then he left the house.

Ten minutes later, he returned. "I'm taking Zoe and Kalina with me. I've arranged protection."

Elaine gave him a cockeyed smile. "I hope it's better than the protection *you* got."

He gave her a wider smile. "It will be. They've caught the leak. A clerk on this end fell in love with a clerk on the other end, and the one on the other end liked to use pillow talk for a little intelligence gathering. That's being cleaned up right now."

He shook his head. "Love. It can cause a brain amputation sometimes."

What the hell was that supposed to mean? Elaine wondered.

But as she watched them drive away in Devlin's rental, she was sure she'd never see him again. Always passing through briefly on the rare occasions he showed at all. Now he was going back to work.

No, they wouldn't see him again for years.

Chapter Twelve

A couple of months had passed since Devlin had left. They'd been good months for the most part. The party of alien watchers had moved on, leaving the streets once again to the locals. The red lights overlooking Beggan Bixby's ranch still hung there most nights but had become so boring nobody bothered to watch them anymore, or even to wonder.

But the exciting news was within the walls of Elaine's house. Kittie had proved to be a miracle. Cassie had spoken a few words to the cat, adding to her repertoire of "Mommy." Then, for the first time ever, she held her arms up for a hug. Not just to be carried to bath and bed but now just for hugs. Once, when Kittie crawled into Elaine's lap, Cassie had followed her.

Huge strides. *Huge.* All because of a little kitten who wasn't quite so little any longer.

Lu's gaze sometimes grew distant, though, as she sat in the evenings in the living room. Elaine suspected she was thinking of Devlin. Wondering how long it would be before she saw him again.

Elaine was more than a little irritated at Devlin for that. It hadn't seemed like such a big thing before, not when it was the usual, not when Caleb was still alive. For some reason, her feelings about that had changed.

What she didn't want to do was admit to herself how much she missed him. How she missed crazy things like the sound of his voice, the fresh, soapy smell of him out of the shower. The way he sometimes looked at her.

The way it had felt the couple of times he'd held her.

Aw, man, she didn't need any complications. She had her job, her daughter. Mostly her daughter, who was at last blossoming a bit and such a joy to be with. Cassie needed every bit of time Elaine could give her. No room for anyone else.

Except she didn't quite believe that no matter how many times she scolded herself about it.

Eventually, though, the silence ended. Without warning at nearly eleven at night. A night when she wasn't on shift. A night when she sat curled up on a chair alone in her living room, an ebook beside her, a glass of white wine beside it.

The knock on the door was quiet. She straightened immediately but before she could rise to answer, the door swung open. In the dim light of the one end-table lamp, she made out the figure of Devlin. She could hardly believe she hadn't fallen asleep into a dream.

"Sorry to come so late."

That was his voice all right. No dream. She pulled her legs from beneath herself and said in a hushed voice, "Devlin?"

"Yeah, the bad penny and all that. Mind?"

He closed the door behind him, though, as if he knew she wouldn't tell him to get lost. Although maybe she should after a couple of months without even a phone call.

He took the recliner across from her. "The two women? We've got them protected in the U.S. until we can figure out how to give them a life back. Thanks for not arresting them."

"Best failure of duty I've ever committed," she said. Her heart was beginning to hammer in her chest. Her mouth began to grow dry. He hadn't come here just to say that. A phone call would have done.

"How's Cassie?" he asked.

"Wonderful. Making great strides. That cat is a miracle."

He smiled. "I am so glad to hear that. And my mother?"

"I think Lu was wondering if you were going to come back. I should go wake her."

He shook his head. "No need. I'll be here in the morning. I'm here to see *you*."

He was? Her heart began to rise into her throat. Breathing grew more difficult, as if the air had been sucked from the room. In a whisper she could barely manage, she said, "Devlin?"

"Well, you probably don't want to hear this, but I've got to say it anyway. While I was gone I realized just how much I missed you. Everything about you. You're strong, stronger than almost anyone I've known. You're a good cop but you've got an even bigger heart. It's just that I missed you. But more than that, I realized I love you. I don't want to be without you.

"So if you can at least give it a little thought, I'd be grateful. And I can promise you I wouldn't be going overseas. Desk job from here on out."

Wow. Just wow. Elaine tried to absorb it all even as her heart lifted with joy. For the first time she faced the feelings that had been developing in her, too. Feelings she'd forced herself to bury beneath guilt, beneath obligation.

Feelings that erupted without hesitation. "I love you, too."

He rose and came over to kneel before her, sliding himself between her legs, wrapping his arms around her waist, encouraging her to rest her head on his shoulder.

"I've never felt this way about anyone," he murmured. "Never, ever. And I don't want to lose you ever. Just say you'll marry me."

"I will." That proved to be the easiest statement in her life.

And it only got better a few minutes later, when Cassie came stumbling down the hallway, rubbing her eyes, Kittie at her side. She stopped and looked at the two of them.

"Devlin," she said, as clear as a bell. Then she walked over and joined the hug.

Elaine thought her heart would stop and never start again. Never had there been a moment more perfect.

* * * * *

Look for more books in New York Times *bestselling author Rachel Lee's incredibly popular miniseries, Conard County: The Next Generation, coming soon!*